YA FIC VOL / T 4718 / Quiz # 87550

Black and white

Reading Level 4.9 / 6 Points

BLACK AND WHITE

BLACK AND WHITE

PAUL VOLPONI

VIKING

VIKING

Published by Penguin Group

Penguin Young Readers Group, 345 Hudson Street, New York, New York 10014, U.S.A.

Penguin Group (Canada), 10 Alcorn Avenue, Toronto,

Ontario, Canada M4V 3B2 (a division of Pearson Penguin Canada Inc.)

Penguin Books Ltd, 80 Strand, London WC2R 0RL, England

Penguin Ireland, 25 St Stephen's Green, Dublin 2, Ireland

(a division of Penguin Books Ltd)

Penguin Group (Australia), 250 Camberwell Road, Camberwell, Victoria 3124,

Australia (a division of Pearson Australia Group Pty Ltd)

Penguin Books India Pvt Ltd, 11 Community Centre, Panchsheel Park,

New Delhi – 110 017, India

Penguin Group (NZ), Cnr Airborne and Rosedale Roads, Albany, Auckland,

New Zealand (a division of Pearson New Zealand Ltd)

Penguin Books (South Africa) (Pty) Ltd, 24 Sturdee Avenue,

Rosebank, Johannesburg 2196, South Africa

Penguin Books Ltd, Registered Offices: 80 Strand, London WC2R 0RL, England

First published in 2005 by Viking, a division of Penguin Young Readers Group

5 7 9 10 8 6

LIBRARY OF CONGRESS CATALOGING-IN-PUBLICATION DATA

Volponi, Paul.

Black and white / by Paul Volponi.

p. cm.

Summary: Two star high school basketball players, one black and one white,
experience the justice system differently after committing a crime
together and getting caught.

ISBN 0-670-06006-2 (hardcover)

1. African Americans—Juvenile fiction. [1. African Americans—Fiction. 2. Race
relations—Fiction. 3. Basketball—Fiction. 4. Juvenile delinquency—Fiction.
5. High schools—Fiction. 6. Schools—Fiction.] I. Title.

PZ7.V8877Bl 2005   [Fic]—dc22   2004024543

Printed in U.S.A.

Set in Memphis and Avenir

Book design by Nancy Brennan

THIS NOVEL IS DEDICATED

to the loving memory of my father.

*He showed me the angles on a basketball court
and how to look inside them.*

*Special thanks to my mother, wife, and daughter,
who kept a place in their hearts warm for me
while I was busy with this work.*

Thanks to the people who helped me along the way to write:
Anthony Cipollone
April Volponi
Bob Fierro
Jim Cocoros
Lenny Shulman
Rosemary Stimola
Jill Davis

BLACK

I admit it. I've been scared shitless lots of times. But I was never as shook as when the gun in Eddie's hand went off. It thundered inside that car like the whole world was coming to an end. I never expected Eddie to pull the trigger, by accident or any other way. I guess that was a big part of it, too. In all the time Eddie had that gun, we never shot it off once. It was just for show, so we could get our hands on some quick money. That's all. We never flashed it around in front of our friends or anything. It was just for us to know about.

I was more scared for that man we shot than anything else. I didn't even know he got clipped in the head until Eddie told me later. The gun went off and I closed my eyes. I shut them so tight, I thought my eyelids would squeeze them right out of their sockets. I only opened them again to find the handle on the door, so I could get out of that car and take off running.

That damn sound was ringing in my ears. There was no way to outrun that. I couldn't hear the air pumping in and out of my lungs, or the sound of my feet hitting against the concrete. And I didn't know that Eddie wasn't right behind me until I was halfway home, and peeked back over my shoulder. Then I looked back for him again, even though I knew he wasn't there.

I ran to my crib on instinct, and I guessed Eddie did the same. But I wished he was right there with me to explain what happened. I had to know right then. My brain was going twice as fast as my feet. I didn't know how to slow it down or what to think about first. I just needed to tell Eddie I had seen that man someplace before. I could still see his round, black face in front of me, like he was somebody I passed on the streets a hundred times. And I was praying to God with every breath I took that the man wasn't dead.

My name is Marcus Brown, but almost everybody outside my family calls me "Black." That's because they're used to seeing me all the time with my boy, Eddie Russo. Eddie is white. Kids who are different colors don't get to be that tight in my neighborhood. But we got past all that racial crap, until we were almost like real blood brothers. So somebody came up with the tag "Black and White" for us, and it stuck. It got more hype because we played basketball and football for Long Island City High School. We were two of the best players they ever had. Everybody who goes there knows about us. We even made the newspapers for winning big games a couple of times. Scouts from lots of colleges came to see us play. Some of them wanted to sign up the both of us, and keep what we had going. But that's all finished with now.

I don't remember if the idea of robbing people came up before Eddie snuck out his dead grandfather's gun or not. But once the two of those things were square in front of us, they fit together right. We weren't trying to get rich off it. We were just looking for enough money to keep up.

Lots of kids we knew either hustled drugs for their loot or pulled little stickups on the street. But drug dealers and ballplayers usually hold down opposite ends of the park, shooting looks at each other over who runs the place. That's how it was for Eddie and me with them.

The football team always had two or three posses that ripped people off. They would wave their dough around at parties and latch on to the best girls. Some of them even bought rides with their money, while Eddie and me wore out the bottoms of our good kicks walking. And whenever those dudes went out to celebrate after a big win, we were like two charity cases. Then word started getting out among the right females that Black and White were strictly welfare.

Eddie's family has more money than mine. They live two blocks down and across the street from the Ravenswood Houses, in a private house with a front porch. Eddie has a mother and a father, and they both work. Eddie gets an allowance that's only a little bigger than what I get to go to school with every week. But if Eddie ever needed twenty bucks for something, he could put his hand out and probably get it. My mother has always been tight like that. The only money coming in is from her sewing jobs, and what the state sends her every month to take care of me and my little sister.

Senior dues were $150, and the end of February was the deadline. You either paid it or missed out on everything good that went along with graduating, like the class trips to Bear Mountain and Six Flags. It took me almost three months to save that kind of money. Eddie put a lock on his wallet, too, and we were just about there.

Then around the middle of January, Nike came out

with the new Marauders. Everybody on the basketball team was buying a pair because they came in maroon and powder blue, the same as our school colors. We were the main attraction on that squad. There was no way we were getting caught behind the times like that. So we spent most of our dough on new basketball kicks. That left us with just over a month to get the money we needed for dues. We didn't know how we'd do it. But we made a pact that either both of us would come up with the cash, or we'd miss out on everything together.

Teenagers can get a job easy in some place like McDonald's or Burger King. It's honest, but it's low-rent, too. Kids at school and around our way already treated us like stars. And we were going to be even bigger one day. First in college, and then the pros. So we decided Black and White shouldn't be serving up fries in those stupid hats for everybody to see. Besides, there was almost no way to juggle going to practice every day and having a job.

That's when Eddie first snuck out the gun, thinking we could sell it. We knew a kid who paid almost $300 for a .38 caliber just like it. But Eddie's father knew where the gun was supposed to be and might go looking for it one day. Eddie couldn't blame something like that on his sister. His father would have known it was him, straight off. So we figured that we could borrow the gun anytime, then put it back. That's how we came to do stickups.

We kicked it around a lot first and knew everything we could lose. But it was only going to be a problem if we got caught. Eddie and me weren't going to be that dumb. We were just going to pull enough stickups to get the money for dues. Then we'd call it quits.

Eddie was sold on the idea before I was. "It'll be too easy," he said. "And whatever we can take, we deserve." That hit something inside, and pushed me over the line.

We knew enough not to rob other kids. They could get stupid right in the middle of it, or might have a posse of their own and come back after us. We were looking for a payday, not a war. Adults are just easier. Most of them don't want any trouble. They're scared of kids they don't know. And unless you get unlucky and try to heist an off-duty cop or corrections officer, you're usually home free. We even thought about taking the bullets out of the gun, just to play it safe. But we stressed, thinking we might have to shoot it off in the air, if there was ever any real drama.

Growing up, kids all around my way would boost

little things from stores, like candy and soda. If you got caught, the owners would beat your ass good before they'd even think about calling the cops. But I was more worried about what my mother would do to me, and how it would make her feel to know her only son was a thief. It wasn't worth it to me back then. I would rather watch everyone else getting over than turn my own mother against me.

But things were different now. I was already seventeen. I had to start pulling my own weight, until playing ball paid off in cash. It was the same for Eddie. He was my best friend, and the only one I would ever trust on something like this.

We practiced coming up on people, over and over. Eddie said we should watch how they did it on TV, because they copied things like that from the way it really goes down. So we worked on it, like any play we ever ran in a game. Then we scouted out a good-sized parking lot just off the end of Steinway Street, where people shopping might have some real cheese on them.

The lot was laid out in front of a P.C. Richards electronics store, and always deep with rows of cars. There was a big hardware store on one side of it, a movie theater on the other, and a pizza restaurant across the street. There was a sign that read, PARKING

FOR P.C. RICHARDS CUSTOMERS ONLY! But we watched, and everyone going into those other places used that lot, too. In between everything, there was a little park without a basketball hoop. It just had kiddie things in it, like a seesaw and a jungle-gym set. It was empty during the day because of the cold, and we knew it would be the same at night. So we used it as a sort of base to look things over.

Our first time out, it took almost an hour before we moved. We sat on the swings going back and forth, figuring out if we had the nerve to pull it off or not. Lots of people walked by alone, but we just watched them all. Then we started dissing each other about who was going to chicken out first. When all that ran dry, we got quiet and moved closer to the gate. We picked out a white lady carrying a shopping bag. She walked real slow. That was good for us because we wanted to keep our timing right. Eddie and me were walking even with each other, maybe twenty feet apart. And if that lady had turned around, she never would have thought we were together.

We waited until she got all the way to her car. Then Eddie came up from behind and showed her the gun. She got hysterical right away and started to cry. I took the package out of her hand so she could open her pocketbook. Her wallet was sitting right on top.

She was so scared, she couldn't pull it out. Finally, Eddie reached in and grabbed it. Then we got our asses out of there quick.

I didn't want to throw the lady's package down in the street and have somebody take a second look at us. So I just held on to it tight, and dropped my face down behind it. We weren't even a block away when she started screaming for help.

I hated the way she sounded. It was like we did something really terrible to her. After that, Eddie and me decided we'd never rob another woman.

"It's like if somebody did that to your mother," Eddie said. "How would you feel?"

I was just happy we got away with it. We were so nervous that almost a half hour went by before we looked in her wallet. There was $92 inside. So we did a little victory dance, and gave each other high fives out behind my building. We looked at the picture on her driver's license for a second, but neither one of us wanted to know her name. Then we walked a couple of blocks and threw her wallet into a big trash bin behind a supermarket, credit cards and all.

There was a brand-new Walkman in the package. Eddie said he wanted me to keep it for acting so smart and holding on to it. I scratched up the cover so it wouldn't look like it was right out of the box. Then

I gave it to my little sister, Sabrina, and told my mother I found it outside of school. Sabrina had the earphones plugged into her head for a week straight. And every time I saw her with it, I thought about what Eddie and me had done.

Two weeks after that, we robbed an old white man just before the stores closed that night. We were about to step to him when somebody passed by out of nowhere. Eddie and me just froze for five or six seconds. When I looked up again the man was already halfway into his car. I was surprised when Eddie went ahead and pulled the gun on him anyway.

Eddie's face turned mean-looking. He made the man slide over, and got into the driver's seat next to him. Then Eddie unlocked the back door, and I got in, too. He screamed at the man to empty all his pockets. I didn't see much because my eyes were glued to the side window, watching for trouble. But after the man took out his money, he had his eyes shut tight. When we bounced, Eddie grabbed the man's car keys and left them on his back bumper.

"The cops probably won't even find them back there," Eddie said.

And we walked away fast with confidence, like we were professionals now.

That job got us $129 in folding money, almost $3 in

loose change and a token to drive across the Triboro Bridge.

I remember, we stopped at the McDonald's underneath the train tracks on Broadway and each had two Quarter-Pounders with Cheese. Then we left the token on the table like a tip for anybody who wanted it.

Between our loot and what we had saved, there was enough for dues. We held on to the money over the weekend just to look at it some more. But when we went to pay that Monday, the school secretary got bent out of shape because it was March first already.

Eddie knows how to fast-talk most people good, and he didn't waste a second after the last word left her mouth. He told her I was busy celebrating Black History Month. That he thought it was a leap year, and February had the one extra day to it. She smiled at all of that nonsense and made us each out a receipt.

We were happy the way everything turned out, but were flat broke again. It all went down too easy to just walk away. And neither one of us mentioned quitting the stickup business.

Our last stickup was on the next Friday night, after basketball practice. Before we left, Coach Casey called everyone over to the bleachers and gave his usual speech for the weekend.

"Gentlemen, I know the city never sleeps, but try not to get into anything stupid over the next couple of days," Casey told the team. "Don't get into fights and don't get locked up. Do your families a favor—stay home at night and study. I want to see everybody back here on Monday the way we left."

Eddie and me would always smile at each other while Casey talked like that. Not because we didn't appreciate it, but because we knew his rap inside out. We heard him make that same speech every Friday for almost four years. But Casey was solid with us. And we knew he meant it.

On our way up to Steinway Street, Eddie asked me if I wanted to be the one to hold the gun this time. It felt good in my hand the couple of times I played around with it. But I didn't have any real practice pulling it out on somebody. Eddie had been perfect twice already. I didn't want to screw things up, so I took a pass.

It was freezing out that night. We started to shiver, waiting in the back of the parking lot, across from the park. We had our eyes locked onto everything around us, looking for somebody easy. We even passed on a man with a cane because it didn't feel right, and the wind came up strong against us.

Eddie said that holding the gun was like squeezing a piece of ice, and his fingers were going numb. So I let him have my gloves. After a while, I started blowing into my hands to keep them warm. I could see my breath coming out between my fingers, and anybody who saw us there probably thought we were smoking weed.

The man was just a shadow to me when he first came out of that hardware store. It was really dark, and he had his coat buttoned all the way up around his neck. Eddie gave me a nod, and I nodded right back. I didn't even know the man was black until we walked up to him, and Eddie told him it was a stickup.

WHITE

By the time I made it home, the sweat was pouring off of me. I was breathing harder than ever. Every part of my body was on fire. I couldn't go inside, or everyone would know something was wrong.

My right hand was in my coat pocket, still wrapped around the gun. I could smell that it had just been fired. But I wouldn't pull it out again.

I bit down hard on the tip of a finger, and pulled Marcus's glove off of my other hand with my teeth. I wiped the sweat from my face with it, and stuffed the glove into the empty coat pocket. I turned the knob on the front door and opened it.

Gotti jumped up and hit me in the stomach with both paws. But I pushed him down with one hand and scratched him behind the ear. My sister was lying on the floor watching TV.

"Isn't Marcus with you?" she asked.

I wasn't sure what would come out of my mouth. So I just shook my head.

My folks were in the kitchen. I heard my mom call out something to me about dinner, but I went right upstairs, and locked the bathroom door behind me. When I turned back around, I was staring straight into the mirror.

The sweat was starting down my forehead again. The skin was stretched tight across my face, and my eyes were bulging out. I could have been looking at a murderer. I took the gun out of my pocket and put it in the sink.

I heard my sister coming up the stairs, talking on the phone. That's when I felt a *bang!* Like I had shot that man all over again. Only I could feel the trigger slip between my finger and Marcus's glove this time. I could feel myself jerk backwards, and could see the blood.

I listened until I heard my sister's bedroom door shut. Then I peeled off the other glove and grabbed the gun. I opened the door just wide enough to check the hall, and when I saw that it was clear, I bolted for the attic.

My mom hadn't changed a thing up there since my grandpa died in his sleep last year. Sometimes, it almost felt like he still lived with us. The pictures of him with my grandma were on the table next to his bed. My mom dusted them almost every day. In all the times I took his gun, it never bothered me. But now I felt sick to my stomach.

I reached up to the top shelf of his closet and took down the brown shoe box. There were a dozen rubber bands wrapped around it. They were old and stiff. But I undid them all without any of them snapping. I had left a brick in its place. So I put the gun back inside, and hid the brick on the closet floor under some old magazines. Then I slipped the rubber bands back around the box, and put it away.

I got out of there and grabbed a basketball from my room. Halfway down the stairs, I held the ball out in front of me to stop any questions about where I was headed. My mom saw me at the bottom step and called out my name. Then my dad turned around to look at me. I lifted the ball up in front of my face and said, "I'm going out to find Marcus."

The wind ran through my wet clothes. I tried to dribble the ball to keep warm. But it would hardly come back up off the ground. It was just too cold. I knew that Marcus would be either in his house or at the courts in the Circle. I turned in between the first two buildings of the projects and could hear a game going on.

I turned the next corner and the wind dropped off behind the big buildings. Moses and X were playing one-on-one at the basket under the light. Marcus was sitting by himself on a bench next to the court. His hands were in his pockets, and his face was down into his coat.

X yelled, "Now we can play some two-man."

When I heard that, I knew that he hadn't told them what happened.

It was the first time I could remember that me and Marcus didn't give each other a pound or a slap on the back. We just looked at each other.

"It just went off," I said to him in a low voice.

I flipped Marcus the ball and he cradled it in his fingertips. He made an excuse to Moses and X about not playing, and we headed out of the other end of the park together.

"Look at them go! They're so scared!" Moses echoed through the Circle.

"They're feeling the pressure, big time," hooted X. "They know it could have been the end of Black and White tonight."

And they both laughed.

When we got out of earshot, Marcus asked me, "Do you think he's dead?"

I told him that I didn't think so. That the bullet just grazed him, and there was blood on the back of his head and neck. I knew the window next to him got shattered. But, I wasn't really sure about anything.

"Oh God, not in the head!" Marcus cried out loud. Then he jumped up and smacked a street sign with the basketball. The sound rattled down the block and I turned around to see if anybody was watching.

We talked about going back there to see what was going on. Maybe there was police tape around the car already and a bunch of cops asking people about what they had seen. We thought we could find out if the man was still alive that way. But in the end, we decided against it.

"What if he's still in the car, and nobody's found him yet?" Marcus asked. "Do we call an ambulance? Do we leave him there?"

"I don't know," I said. "I can't think straight."

So we just kept walking in circles around the projects.

Then Marcus said, "I thought I recognized that man from somewhere."

I told him that he was just imagining things. But he said how that could have been the father of some kid he knew, and his eyes started to tear.

"I know I fucked this up for us, and got that man shot. I shoulda took the gun when you asked. I punked out!" Marcus said.

I didn't want to hear any more, so I started to walk off. Marcus grabbed my shoulder to turn me back around. That's when he saw the blood on my coat. I rubbed the spots hard with spit and some napkins I found up against the curb. But it wouldn't come off.

And I wasn't about to take it home for my mom to wash.

We ditched the coat into an open trash bag out behind White Castle. I tied the bag up tight with two strong knots. The gloves looked clean, but we didn't want to hold on to them, or leave them in the same place as my coat. So we stuffed them down a sewer on the next street corner.

I was freezing. But I couldn't go home without a coat, or somebody might put two and two together. Marcus took me back to his place. We were always trading jackets anyway, so I'd be able to get away with that. But as soon as I walked in the door his mother asked me, "Where's your coat, child?"

I told her that I took it off to play ball and somebody walked away with it.

"What some kids won't do to get what they want," she said, shaking her head.

It was almost like lying to my own mother. But before it got any worse, Marcus came out with another jacket and told her that he was going to walk me home.

"Don't you boys go looking for who took that coat now," she said. "Just let it go. Maybe some poor child needs it to keep warm. It's cold as the devil out there."

I promised her that we wouldn't, and Marcus said

he'd come straight home. After we left, we didn't say a word to each other for a while. I knew how terrible I felt. But I knew that Marcus was feeling even worse than I did. Maybe because that man was black, too.

We passed back through the Circle, and it was empty.

Everybody calls that park the Circle because it's right in the middle of the Ravenswood Houses, surrounded by the buildings on every side. I'd been playing there since I was thirteen. Marcus brought me down after we met at the courts on 21st Street, over by the Department of Sanitation. I'm the only white kid that hangs out there. Nobody took to me right away. I had to fight plenty of times before I got any respect. But the Circle is where "Black and White" was born. And now we ran that court because nobody else could deal with the two of us.

I stopped us on the corner of my block. I didn't need to take Marcus inside with me and risk having to answer any more questions. So we clamped our hands together, and gave each other a pound. But it didn't feel like usual.

I got into the house and up to my room without having to say a word to anybody.

B L A C K

Every time I shut my eyes that night, I saw the man's face. The shadows moved around under my eyelids until he came out clear. I'd look over every line and bump. And sometimes, he'd stare straight back at me. I couldn't figure out where I knew him from. But seeing his face that way made me feel like he was still alive.

I wouldn't go out of the house for anything the next day. I watched the news on TV and listened to the radio, waiting for a story about a man who got killed in a Queens stickup. But there was nothing.

Eddie didn't call me at all that day. I didn't dial his digits, either. I helped my sister with her homework and folded some clothes in my room. When my mother saw that I wasn't going out that night, she asked, "What's got you pinned down inside this apartment on a Saturday night?"

I looked at her like I didn't know what she was talking about.

"Let me hear it!" she demanded.

I told her I was saving my strength for the game against Grover Cleveland on Tuesday night. That at least three or four college scouts would be there, and maybe I'd finally pick a school. But she didn't buy that.

"I just hope it's a girl you're hiding out from, and not some street gang," she said, straight out.

Eddie's sister, Rose, called me on Sunday. They had cousins visiting from Long Island and were taking them to the movies. Her mother was making Eddie go, too, because it was family. So Rose invited me, too. She even talked her mother into buying my ticket.

I had it bad for Rose, and thought she felt the same. She would kiss me on the cheek almost every time I saw her. And when Eddie wasn't around, she'd catch the corner of my lips, and give me a sexy smile. Rose went to school at LIC with Eddie and me, but was a year behind us.

Eddie caught me staring at her from behind one time. I didn't know how to pretend that I wasn't, so I didn't even try to come up with an excuse. He just shook his head and said, "Don't even think about it, Black! Don't even think about it!"

I never thought about going out with a white girl before. Every girl I ever went out with was black. But my best friend was white. So I didn't see the difference.

Eddie rang me a half hour after Rose, worried to death. He said Rose and the cousins wanted to see something that was playing at Kaufman Studios. That was just across the street and down the block from where we shot that man. He tried to talk them into seeing another flick or going to a different theater. But they wouldn't budge.

I was nervous about going back there, too. But I cupped my hands around the phone and told him it would be all right. That maybe we could find out what happened.

We met at the bus stop across the street from my house, just after four o'clock. Their cousins had never seen the projects before, and were looking around like they had just landed on another planet. Rose showed them the police station built right into one of the buildings. There were a couple of squad cars and some scooters parked outside. I gave Rose a wink and said, "Without those cops on scooters, it would be a jungle out here."

Rose was laughing under her breath. But Eddie wouldn't smile. I tried to keep him loose, but something was pulling hard at me, too. I had to know where I saw that man before. I kept thinking I had it.

But it would slip out of my head with the sound of every car that zipped past.

The buses run slower than snails on Sunday. And it was brick outside, wind and all. For a second, I thought about putting on my gloves. Then it sunk in all over again.

The Number 66 bus finally showed. I lifted my leg for the first step, and something settled in my brain. I could feel my insides go numb. But I kept on climbing. By the time I reached the top and heard Eddie's change going into the box, I knew the man we shot was a driver on the 19-A that ran past my house. I looked up and could see his black face pasted on the man who was driving.

Rose wanted to sit up front, but I pushed everyone as far back as I could. Then the bus started to roll again, and we all had to grab fast for something to hold on to. There were plenty of seats, but I wouldn't sit down for anything. I stood up with both hands wrapped around the silver rail over my head. The sweat was starting down my face, and I felt sick to my stomach. I thought I was going to throw up.

I almost never rode the bus. So I didn't know how I remembered that driver. I could walk to school in the time it took to wait on the 19-A in the morning. I'd get on with my mother to go shopping, and took it with the team to the subway station when we had road games. There was no way he could have remembered me. He probably saw a thousand people get on and off his bus every day. But I remembered him.

The bus turned off 21st Street, and started down 35th Avenue to Kaufman Studios. Eddie was staring out the window. I wanted to tell him about it, but everyone was between us. When Eddie finally looked up, I pushed my jaw out at him like it was going to explode. He leaned over to me. But Rose said my name out loud, and we both backed off.

We got to our stop and I went straight for the back door. The cold wind dried my sweat. And I felt better with every step on the solid concrete. I grabbed Eddie around the shoulder and pulled him off to the side.

"He's a bus driver from right around here," I whispered to him. "I know it now. I've been on his bus."

Eddie slipped out from under my arm. Then he turned back to me and said, "He had to be somebody."

It was less than a block before we had to turn on the next street and see that parking lot. I raised my eyes and saw the sign for the movie. The lights were turned up bright, and there was a flashing neon arrow pointing around the corner.

I couldn't look. So I watched Eddie's face as we turned. His eyes zeroed in on the lot. Then he looked back at me with a face that was almost normal. That's when I checked it out for myself. The car wasn't there. There was no police tape or crime scene marked off. There weren't any flowers or crosses that get put up when somebody dies out on the street. It was all calm, like nothing jumped off there two nights ago.

Next thing I knew Rose was buying the movie tickets. I recognized the kid working the door from school. He ripped our tickets in half and gave us back the stubs. He looked up at us and said, "Black and White, enjoy the show!"

Eddie nodded his head to me, and put a big smile across his face. We found the theater where the movie was playing. The lights went out just before we got to our seats. The two cousins went into the row first. Then I followed behind Rose, with Eddie sitting on the end.

We saw *The Count of Monte Cristo*. Rose and the cousins were the ones who picked it out. They said that sooner or later, everybody had to read that book for school, so why not see the movie first. I really got into the story and almost forgot about everything else. Eddie started to ease up, too. I heard him pulling hard for the hero during the sword fight scenes. I took turns with Rose sharing the armrest between seats, and sometimes our elbows fit in together.

When we left, Eddie took us around the far corner, away from the parking lot. The last time Eddie and me were on those streets in the dark, we were running in different directions. But everything was all right now. We were side by side, breathing easy. Everybody was talking about the movie, and how much they liked it. None of us could believe how one friend turned on the other that way, especially Eddie. But we all thought it was right on the money how that bastard got what was coming to him.

We swung back around to 35th Avenue, but there was no bus in sight. So we started walking. We were two or three stops down, when one finally came up behind us. Eddie and me looked at each other for a second. Then we dropped our heads, until we saw that the bus driver was white.

That night, I dreamed about my father. He left right after my sister was born; I hadn't seen him since I was a little kid. My mother was so pissed that she didn't keep a single picture of him. So I didn't have a handle on what he looked like anymore. In my dreams, I was always looking straight ahead. And he was standing next to me, with a hand on my shoulder.

My dreams about him were always the same. We'd be in the park or someplace thick with trees. Then we'd laugh about something and start to race. I'd run as fast as I could, and I could feel him right behind me. No matter how tired I got, I'd keep pushing myself. I'd wake up from those dreams the same way every time—breathing hard with my heart pounding.

The next morning, I walked the side streets to school, off the bus route. Eddie and me never left for school together. We tried it for a while, two years back. But one of us always wound up waiting on the other and getting steamed.

I didn't see Eddie until third period, in English class. Ms. Sussman was our teacher, and assigned us seats on opposite sides of the room. Eddie and me had her once before as freshmen, so she was wise to our act and wouldn't let us sit together.

I was already copying the work on the board when Eddie got there just after the bell. Ms. Sussman gave him a late mark, and he didn't argue. Eddie would always try to change her mind with some story. But he just took the hit.

We caught each other's eye a couple of times during class. Then Eddie cracked a joke off some kid's stupid answer. He turned straight towards me to laugh. I howled right along with him, until Ms. Sussman gave us both a zero.

Eddie's mother was checking program cards on the way into the cafeteria. She worked at LIC as a school aide. She used to be in our old junior high school, too. Then she transferred over when Rose got here.

"This is my second son," she told the teacher working the door with her. "He's my illegitimate second son," she said, hugging me around the neck.

Eddie's mother was always playing around like that. She'd tell people about me, "He watches my TV, he eats my pasta and he doesn't give me a dime for any of it. He must be my other son. My Black-Italian son from Sicily. That's just a stone's throw from Africa."

It didn't bother Eddie one bit that his mother worked in our school. I love my mother more than anything, but I wouldn't want to be running into her in the halls, or have her hanging around my teachers. Nobody would. But Eddie didn't act any different around his mother. He was always the same, either way. And I respected him for that.

We finished the day in math class together. The teacher there had assigned seats, too. Eddie sat right in front of me. Math was always the hardest subject for Eddie, but he had to pass to play ball. I knew my formulas cold and helped him study. When we had multiple-choice tests, Eddie would lay his pen down on any problem that had him stumped. Then I'd kick the back of his chair to let him know what answer I had. It was always one kick for "A," two for "B," and three for "C."

After class, we went up to the gym to basketball practice. Our lockers were right next to each other, and we took our time changing. We knew that Casey wouldn't run us hard because of the game the next night. Casey was the head basketball coach and an assistant coach on the football team. He did everything he could to make sure none of his basketball players got banged up too bad during football season, especially Eddie and me.

Casey got college scholarships for lots of kids from our neighborhood. But none of them made it to the pros yet. That's where Black and White was going to be different. We were both going to make it big. That's why schools like St. John's, Connecticut, and Michigan State were drooling over the both of us.

Coach opened practice with a fifteen-minute shoot-around. Kids were at every basket, getting loose and feeling their favorite shots. Everybody had their own rock to shoot with. And for a while, it was raining basketballs. Then Casey ran us through all our set plays, until we got each one right. He ended practice with a half hour of foul shooting. Everybody paired up at different baskets. And the freshmen had to go downstairs to the girls' gym when we ran out of hoops.

Eddie and me took the main basket in front of Casey's office. We switched on and off, taking twenty foul shots apiece and chasing the ball down for the shooter. We started off okay. But by the third time around, we both found the groove. I knocked down eighteen out of twenty shots. Then Eddie stepped to the line and made twenty straight. It felt like everything was almost back to the way it was. And the only sound in my head was the ball slipping through the net.

We walked home together after practice, and talked about how lucky we got. Eddie and me were sure the man was still alive, or else we would have heard something on the news. And since that whole mess blew up in our faces, we almost forgot about picking a college.

Eddie thought we should both stay in New York

and play at St. John's. "Black and White on the back page of every New York newspaper for the next four years," Eddie said, "unless we turn pro early."

That sounded like a sweet deal. I had never been away from home before, and didn't want my mother and sister to be alone. So I was hyped.

I put an echo into my voice, like an announcer, and said loud, "Keeping it real in the Big Apple. From the Circle in the Ravenswood Houses to Alumni Hall at St. John's University. All of N-Y-C, rec-og-nize Eddie Russo and Marc—"

But I broke down laughing before I could finish.

My mother had dinner waiting for me on a plate under some tin foil. She was helping Sabrina practice for the fifth-grade spelling bee. I sat in the kitchen, eating and listening to my sister spell out loud from the living room. I closed my eyes and took a deep breath. When I opened them again, everything was still all right.

WHITE

When I got home, my dad was waiting for me. He had a serious look on his face and wanted to talk. I was sure that he knew about the gun.

"Let me tell you something about your grandpa," he started off, as I fixed my feet to the floor. "He worked almost forty years for the Department of Sanitation, and got me the job there, too, right before I married your mother. It's an okay job. It pays the bills, and it got us this house. But things are going to be different for you. You've got a real chance in life. Sports are going to get you into college for sure. But I want you to pick a school where you're going to learn something, and not just play ball. I want you to study and get a diploma. That way you'll always be somebody, no matter what happens. Then you'll never have to lift garbage cans for a living like your old man."

He showed me the dark lines in his palms where the dirt got in so deep it wouldn't wash out. Then he slipped a hand around the back of my neck and pulled me into a bear hug.

Before he let me go, he looked up at the attic and said, "If your grandpa ever heard me talk like that about the job that feeds us, he'd have taken a strap to me. And I still have to be careful about what I say, in case he's listening from up there."

I couldn't fall asleep that night. Little noises in the house had me jumping, and Gotti kept barking at something. Every time I opened my eyes, I thought I saw Grandpa's shadow. The next morning, I woke up with my head under the covers, soaked in sweat, and didn't feel right until I was outside and on my way to school.

The cheerleaders came looking for me during homeroom to set up a party for after the game. Rebecca Coles was there. She was the captain of their squad.

I didn't have a girlfriend. But if I did, I guess it would have been Rebecca. We had hooked up a couple of times since last year, and she was always cool about letting it lay low. She just walked up to me after a game one time and said that she couldn't stop thinking about me. It doesn't get any easier than that for a guy. But I liked her, too. Rebecca can throw a perfect spiral with a football. She said she used to play with her older brothers, until she started thinking about boys all the time.

I couldn't even think about a party until after we won that night.

"You can't talk to him now. He's got his game face on already," Rebecca said, punching me in the stomach.

I picked my hands up without thinking. Then she stepped back and smiled.

"What are you gonna to do to me, tough guy?" she laughed, dancing around like a boxer. "Are you going to knock my block off and go to jail instead of playing in the game tonight? Is that what you want?" she went on, trying to keep a straight face.

I was laughing, too, until she said the part about jail.

After last period, I went straight up to the gym, spread a towel over one of the benches in the locker room, and tried to catch some sleep. But just as I started to get comfortable, the kids on the track team showed up to change for their practice. That woke me up. So I put on my uniform and grabbed a basketball from the rack.

The game wasn't for another two hours, and the bleachers hadn't even been pulled out yet. I ran up and down the court pretending the gym was packed. I would take the pass from Marcus and could hear the crowd roaring in my head when I drove for the hoop. I could see my family in the stands. They were cheering louder than anybody. Everything was like it was supposed to be.

But when I stopped pretending, there I was, alone.

I went back to the locker room, and some of our guys were already there. Andre was our big man in the middle. He was just a junior, but he was six-foot-seven and still growing.

"Yo, White," he said with a smile. "Thanks for not picking a school yet. I love that all these scouts are still coming out to see you and Black play. That means they're all getting a peek at me for next year. Good looking out for a teammate."

That's when Marcus came in with Moses and X.

"Ravenswood Projects are in the house!" X screamed.

Marcus slapped my hand and said, "Big night for Black and White, my brother!"

Then Moses grabbed a freshman named Preston, and told him he was on the door tonight. That meant he had to wait for the Grover Cleveland team to show, and bring them up the back stairs to the visitors' locker room. Preston got really pissed off. He had the door the last time we played a home game.

"I just dig having a white doorman," snapped X.

Besides me, Preston was the only other white player on the team. He wasn't bad for a freshman. But he played guard, like me and Marcus. So he never got into the game, unless it was a blowout.

"We want them to see your skinny freshman ass first," Moses piped in. "Then when they come out and see the real players—*pow!*—they'll be in shock."

Everyone except for Preston cracked up.

If Marcus was hanging around the locker room when the other squad showed up, he'd always go to the door. He'd show them the way in and shake everybody's hand. He was totally the opposite of me. I didn't want to talk to anybody on the other team or shake their hand until the game was over.

When we were still in junior high school, me and Marcus used to sneak up those same stairs to see the games. Jason Taylor was the LIC captain back then. He lived in the projects and knew us from the Circle. We used to bang on the door while he was waiting for the other team, and he'd let us up. Then over one Christmas vacation, the team went up to Albany to play in a tournament. The newspapers said that things got tense on the court, and there was a lot of racial shit coming out of the stands. A fight broke out and the whole gym went zoo. They showed the videotape of it on TV for a week. A white kid watching the game ripped the leg off a chair and stabbed Jason through the back with it. He died right there on the court, in Casey's arms. It's something that Coach never talks about.

I don't know when a scrub started letting the other squad up instead of the captain. But that's the way it is now. Besides, we don't have a captain. This team belongs to me and Marcus. Though if it ever came down to choosing, Marcus might pull a few more votes than me.

Casey got us all together before we went out on the court.

"Stay focused out there," he told the team. "Play our normal game and forget about impressing the scouts. Depend on your teammates, and know you've got each other's backs out there."

There were just two games left in the regular season. We were in first place in our division with a record of 16–2. That was good enough to give us home court advantage all the way through the playoffs. Grover Cleveland had lost more games than they won. We beat them by twenty points when we played at their gym a couple of weeks ago.

We put our hands into a big pile. Then everybody counted to three, and shouted, "T-E-A-M!"

Right off, we jumped out to an 8–0 lead. Marcus was getting me the ball the second I broke open, and I hit my first two shots. Neither one of them even touched the rim. They were nothing but net. Then Marcus faked a pass in my direction. When his man slid over, Marcus drove to the hoop alone for an easy score.

Out of the corner of my eye I could see my sister Rose sitting behind our bench with her friends. My mom and dad liked to sit in the last row away from all the noise. So they were impossible to find.

The other team finally made a couple of baskets, but there was no way they could keep up. We were outrunning them up and down the court. I could hear the kid who was guarding me gasping for air. It was 14–4 and their coach was starting to make substitutions already.

I knew at least three of the college scouts by sight. And when the ball kicked out of bounds, I was face-to-face with one of them in the first row. I tried not to notice him. I took the ball from the ref and passed it back in.

Marcus's mother missed most of our games. She always had sewing to finish. I'd listen to Marcus fill her in on how we did. But he never made it sound important enough. So I'd give her my own play-by-play.

"Come to me for the real highlights," I'd tell her. "Marcus is too modest."

The ball popped loose and Marcus grabbed it. He found me running up ahead of everyone. I dunked the ball hard with one hand. I could feel the rim shaking as I let go of it. The cheerleaders were starting up again.

On my way back up court, I flashed Rebecca a big smile.

We rolled through the rest of the first half, and went into halftime leading 43–18. Everything was on cruise control.

It's great in the locker room at halftime when you're kicking ass out on the court. Everyone is all charged up, and nobody minds that the place stinks from the smell of sweat. Not when you're winning big, and the stands outside are still rocking for you.

Andre and X were already talking up their best plays. Even kids who didn't get into the game yet sounded like they had something to do with the score. Marcus was sitting down with a towel over his shoulders. I was walking back and forth trying to keep a good sweat going, and so I wouldn't get stiff.

Casey came in and told us not to get carried away by the score.

"We made a lot of mistakes out there," Casey said. "If we were playing a better team, it might have cost us."

He went over to the chalkboard and put up the plays he wanted to run in the second half. But before he got through, the principal, Ms. Randolph, called Casey from just outside the door. He kept talking to us as he made his way over. Then he tossed the chalk to X, and went outside. That's when X started giving his own speech, and wrote "Take No Prisoners" up on the board.

After a while, Coach called us out for the second half, and we started to run a layup line to get warm. I was looking around at the crowd and the gym like they belonged to me. That's when I noticed that Marcus wasn't out on the court. I thought maybe he hit the bathroom or needed to get taped up, and after another run through the line, I went to check.

I looked back inside the locker room and two guys in suits were handcuffing Marcus. Casey and Ms. Randolph saw me at the door and pushed me back outside. Then Casey wiped a tear from his eye and huddled everybody up around our bench.

"Marcus was just arrested," Casey said, steadying himself. "I can't say why. There's nothing we can do for him right now, except play the rest of the game like it means something to us."

After we broke the huddle, kids were looking at me for answers. But I didn't have anything to say. My legs got weak, and I thought I was going to pass out. I tried not to look anyone in the eye, and walked onto the court. Then the ref blew the whistle to start play.

We beat Grover Cleveland 73–58 that night. I was the high-scorer with thirty-five points.

BLACK

The bus driver's name was Sidney Parker. He remembered me taking the bus with the team from school. The cops got him a copy of our yearbook, and he picked my picture out cold. At least I knew for sure he was alive.

The detectives read my rights to me. The tall one had it all memorized. He bent over every word, like he really enjoyed it. But I was looking at the faces of Casey and Ms. Randolph more than I was listening. I was wondering what they thought about me, especially Coach.

The cops searched my locker for the gun. The older one pulled out a shirt my mother sewed. He went in and out of every pocket. I could feel my mother standing right next to me, waiting to put her foot up my ass. This was going to be the saddest day of her life, only she didn't have a clue yet.

I changed into my street clothes, and they cuffed me. We went down the back staircase. The same one

Jason used to let Eddie and me come up to see the games when we were younger. I remember wanting to wear an LIC jersey just like him. All the way down, I was thinking how Jason was killed in that game upstate. Everybody on the tape was running in different directions. You couldn't make out a thing until the TV station put a white spot on the kid stabbing him with the chair leg. It didn't make any sense. They didn't have any beef. Jason was playing ball, and that kid was sitting in the stands, ready to blow.

People around my way said it was because of that natural hatred. That line between blacks and whites that can't get erased, no matter what. I just remember hating that kid's guts because of what he did to Jason, not because he was white. And everybody I knew—no matter what color—hated him, too.

We reached the bottom, and the detectives pushed the door open. I expected to see Jason standing on the other side, wearing his uniform with the "C" for "captain" on his chest. I knew he'd be shaking his head over everything Eddie and me got mixed up in.

The door swung open fast. It slammed hard against the red brick wall outside. I flinched. But no one was there. The street was empty, and the cops walked me over to their car.

The detectives did most of the talking on the ride to the station. I knew enough from watching police shows on TV to wait for a lawyer before I said too much. But they kept dogging me about my partner. And when I wouldn't answer, they started calling him "the shooter."

"Are you going to take the fall for this alone, while the shooter walks?" the tall one asked me.

"He must be a real good friend of yours, if you don't want to give him up," said the older one. "Who are your two or three closest friends, Marcus? Because if you don't tell us, other people will."

Eddie must have been in a real panic, stressing over getting nabbed, too. The cops already had me. And I didn't have to keep pretending it never happened. I was just worried sick about my mother. At first, she wouldn't believe it, no matter what anybody said. She'd think it was some kind of mix-up with somebody who looked like me. Then I'd have to tell her.

When we got to the precinct, Casey's wife had just come in, too. She told me not to worry. That my mother was on her way, and that Coach would be there for me as soon as he could. I should have told her to go back to the game, and to tell Casey not to come because I wasn't worth the trouble. But I just stood there with my mouth shut until the cops hustled me upstairs.

They took me to a small room with a desk, two wooden chairs, and a phone. Then they handcuffed me to one of the chairs and left. The only window in the room was cut into the wall on my left side. It was completely blacked out, and I knew the cops were probably watching me from the other side. I tried hard not to look over there. But when I did, I was looking into a black mirror. I tested the sound of my voice, and listened to it echo through the room. For a second, I thought I said Eddie's name out loud, and held my breath over that, thinking the cops must be listening in.

The detective with the gray hair came back and asked me a bunch of easy questions in a quiet voice. He wanted to go over my name and where I went to school. He asked about my family, and what I liked to do for fun. Then he took out the school yearbook and found me in the team pictures for football and basketball. The smile never left his face when he asked if a kid on one of those teams was my partner.

He asked if I knew the names Wanda Lang or William Mathes. But before I could answer, he said, "You should, Marcus. Those are the two people you and your partner robbed before Mr. Parker."

That felt like a sucker punch in the gut. He didn't smile or anything over it. His face just stayed even. He started tapping his pencil on the table, and maybe five minutes went by without either one of us saying a word. Then the phone rang. He listened for a few seconds and said, "So he's absolutely sure."

He put the phone down and pointed to the dark window next to my chair.

"Mr. Parker has just made a positive ID on you," said the detective. "He says that without a doubt you were the one in the backseat of his car that night."

I didn't have an answer for him, and sunk even lower into the chair.

I turned and looked hard into that window. I wished I could see Parker's face in it. I was scared as anything to meet him again and hear what he might say. Still, I wanted him to know how sorry I was. But there was no way to get through. No matter how hard I looked, it was just my reflection in that window. And all I could see was my own black face.

The detective started to press me more about who I was with that night. He ran down a bunch of kids' names to me, one by one. I wouldn't shake my head "no" or say anything about them. But he kept going down the list anyway. I knew sooner or later he would get to Eddie's name. I tried to get ready. I grabbed onto the thin arms of the chair until my knuckles turned white. When he finally said, "Eddie Russo," a fire shot through my body. My mouth turned bone dry, and I could feel the sweat on my temples.

They wouldn't let my mother talk to me, and I was almost happy about that. But when they were taking me out, I saw her down at the end of the hallway. She was sitting with Casey and his wife, and jumped up the second she saw me. I could see how scared she was for me. She looked straight at me for some kind of answer, or something she could do. My chest got real tight. I knew I was breathing, but I couldn't say for sure any air was getting through. Then the detective turned me in the other direction. I remember looking back over my shoulder at her, like I belonged in handcuffs.

WHITE

Rose found out from somebody in the crowd that Marcus got arrested. She was in tears, and all over me to tell her what I knew. Some of the kids were saying Marcus probably got into a fight with somebody at school, who went to the cops about it. Only I couldn't stop looking over my shoulder, waiting for the cops to show up again and just haul me away.

Casey left the second the refs blew the whistle to end the game. A few of the scouts were waiting around by his office door, trying to find out what happened to Marcus. The scout from St. John's had talked to me a couple of times before, and once with me and Marcus together. But I didn't have much time left now.

I thought about Marcus being at the police station. And everything I could lose. I had a ticket to play big-time college ball in my hand. I wasn't going to just give it away. So I walked straight up to the scout and told him I wanted to play for St. John's.

"That's great news, Eddie! We've had a scholarship

with your name on it for a while now," he said, handing me his card. "Fax us a letter of intent in the morning, and we'll make it all official."

Then he asked me where Coach was, and why Marcus didn't come out for the second half. Before I had time to open my mouth, one of the other scouts came over to tell him that Casey was gone. I sprinted for the locker room before things got any worse.

I put my street clothes on over my uniform, and went down the same back stairs where the cops took Marcus. Kids on the team saw that I didn't want to talk. They probably thought I was in a hurry to help out my best friend.

A police car passed me on the street, and I just stood frozen until it rolled out of sight. I could feel my heart pounding inside my chest. I knew that Marcus wouldn't point a finger at me. But he might say the wrong thing by mistake, or the cops might trick him into saying we were together that night.

I beat my family back home. They probably waited around for me at the gym. And that was all the head start I needed. I ran up to the attic with Gotti on my heels. I took the shoe box down from the closet, and sat on the edge of my grandpa's bed with it. He had that gun to protect his family. I used it to rob people. The pictures of him with my grandma were looking right at me. I told him how I screwed up, and that I never meant to shoot anybody. But he just stared back at me from every angle.

I opened the box with my hands shaking. I hated the idea of touching that damn gun again. So I held my breath, and grabbed it fast. The gun felt heavier in my hand than it ever had before.

It was always chilly in the attic. And the gun hadn't warmed up a bit since I put it back that night. I closed my palm around the handle with my finger way off the trigger. The cold ran up my arm, and sent a shiver through my spine. I stuffed the gun into the front of my pants and started breathing again. I put the shoe box back with the brick inside. Then I hustled my ass out of the house, taking Gotti with me this time. I wanted to look more like a kid walking his dog than somebody trying to ditch a gun.

I walked up to the projects, and past Marcus's building. Then I turned straight down 21st Street for Astoria Park. Every half block or so, I tapped on the gun to make sure it was still there. The Department of Sanitation garage was on the other side of the street. My dad picked up his truck there in the morning and dropped it off in the same spot every night. My grandpa did the same thing before him for almost forty years.

The park right next to it was where me and Marcus

first played ball together. It's not much of a park, just two full courts laid out side by side. It doesn't have a bench, a water fountain, or a single tree. And in the middle of summer, there isn't any shade at all. That park doesn't even have a name. Everybody just calls it the D.S., because it's right over the fence from the garage.

My old junior high school came up on my side, and I thought about all the fun me and Marcus had there. I waited for the light to change and crossed over at the next corner. The C-Town supermarket was right in front of me. Gotti went wild barking at the big plaster cow and chicken on the roof. And I yanked hard on his choker to get him to stop.

I checked on the gun again, and walked faster.

There's a little graveyard that pops up out of nowhere, right on the street between a tire shop and somebody's house. It takes up the space of a regular-sized building. You can see the whole thing from front to back through the fence. None of the headstones are standing up straight anymore. The graves are so old that the city can't dig them up. But the gate is always locked, and nobody can go inside to visit, either.

I crossed under the Triboro Bridge and into Astoria Park. I walked across the running track where we used to run laps for football practice. One time, we had almost fifty kids there doing laps, when a white dude called another kid a nigger. The black kid tackled him on the spot. Everybody else started pairing off, and choosing sides. Me and Marcus grabbed a hold of each other and were just dancing around in circles. There was almost a riot. But we had fun, and just laughed at everybody.

Shore Boulevard is at the bottom of a short, steep hill. There were only a handful of people hanging out along the strip there. And a few more were in cars, either getting high or making out. I looked over the railing. The East River was rolling up onto the rocks in little waves. But twenty yards out, the currents were really moving.

I walked all the way down to the Hell Gate Bridge before I found an open spot where nobody was watching. The Hell Gate is up on concrete columns as tall as Marcus's building. And it would take an earthquake to shake them. Only freight trains and Amtrak use that bridge. So it's mostly dark and quiet up on the tracks, and the same way underneath.

I wrapped Gotti's leash around the rail, and took a second look around. Then I took a deep breath, and pulled out the gun. I squeezed the handle and threw it as far as I could. I heard the splash, and felt the muscles in my arm start to burn from the strain. Gotti's head was hanging over the rail. He bird-dogged the gun all the way into the water. He didn't want to give up on it, either. But I dragged him back the way we came.

When I got home, everyone was waiting for me. They thought I was at the police station trying to find out what happened to Marcus. It didn't even hit them that Gotti wasn't in the house. I walked in the door with him, and they almost couldn't believe it.

"Where were you?" Rose said, before my mom could get out the same words.

I told them that I just had to get out and think for a while. Then I asked if they had heard anything new about Marcus.

"I called his house," said Rose. "His mother went down to the police station, and there's a neighbor staying with his sister."

"I'm just glad you're not mixed up in any of this," my dad said.

"It's where Marcus lives," my mom jumped in. "It's the projects. There's crime all around him. It was probably just too big a temptation."

Then she took a short, quick breath and said, "Listen to me. I'm talking like he's guilty of whatever it is. Maybe it was some other black boy who looks like him."

I wanted to stop all the talk about Marcus, so I told them that I took the scholarship to St. John's. My mom was so happy she started to cry. Mostly because I wouldn't be moving away.

"I told everybody he would be a success," my dad said at the top of his lungs.

Rose asked me if Marcus getting arrested would stop schools from wanting him, too. "What does that have to do with me?" I snapped.

"Nothing!" my dad said. "Not a thing!"

Rose stared back at me.

Maybe I was the worst friend in the whole world, getting myself into a school while Marcus was in hand-cuffs. But I threw up my arms and walked away from her.

I thought the day I picked a school would be one of the happiest times in my life. That there would be some kind of big celebration at home. I thought me and Marcus would be at a party with the rest of the team. That maybe I would celebrate in private with Rebecca, or some other girl, that night. But here it was, and it was nothing like that.

It took me almost an hour to type out a simple let-ter, saying that I was choosing St. John's.

I spent the whole next morning at school dodging questions about Marcus. I got to homeroom as late as I could. But the second I walked through the door, every-body wanted to know what happened. Most of them

looked shocked when I told them that I didn't know anything. They were asking me about Marcus like I was his
brother. Maybe they thought I was supposed to chase
the cops all the way down to the station house.

Rebecca wasn't asking me to explain anything. But
she talked to me like somebody in my family was sick in
the hospital. I hated that kind of sympathy, especially
because I didn't deserve it. I was going to tell her about
the scholarship, but I couldn't find a place to start.
Every time I brought it up into my throat, it didn't feel
right.

Later, my mom tracked me down in the hall. I could
see in her face that something was wrong. She was
holding the letter I gave her to fax over to St. John's. I
thought the scout had changed his mind and sent it
back. But my mom gave me the letter and said, "It's all
done, and I'm very proud of you."

Then she put her hand on my shoulder and said, "I
went to the principal's office to fax that. Ms. Randolph
told me all about Marcus. Eddie, he was arrested for a
robbery with a gun, and somebody got shot. Can you
believe it?"

She asked me if I was going to be all right. I told her
I could handle it, and that she should worry more about
Rose.

"You're right," she said. "I'm going to find her now.

I don't want her hearing about this from the kids."

She kissed me on the cheek, like that would protect me from something. Then she walked off to find my sister. I could hear the sound of her footsteps behind me when I realized that she said, "Somebody got shot," and not killed.

No matter what happened now, at least it wasn't murder. That man didn't get killed. And I wouldn't have to live with something like that forever.

All through English class, I kept looking over at Marcus's empty seat. I wondered where the cops had him, and what was happening. Marcus could be real strong. I knew he wouldn't break down, not even under those bright lights they use to make people talk.

I knew that Rose would call Marcus's house when she got home. I could get the scoop that way, and find out what was going on. I didn't know if his mother was going to think that I had something to do with it. Marcus knew tons of guys in the projects who could pull something like that. Some of them even had police records. But she knew how much time we spent together.

Marcus had the seat behind me in math. So once I sat down, I just didn't turn around. I tried to block him out of my head and concentrate on the problems on the board. But after a while, I could almost feel him breathing down my neck. I turned around all at once, and almost lost it when I saw a black face staring back at me. Some kid from a couple of rows back had moved up to see the board better. And I almost jumped down his throat.

I went up to the gym after class, but Casey wasn't around. There was just a note on his office door that read, PRACTICE CANCELED TODAY. I don't even think he came to school that day because the note wasn't in his handwriting.

The team was hanging around, talking about it.

"Do you think Coach is out looking after Marcus?" Andre asked out loud.

"No doubt," said Moses, eying me. "Coach is his *real* white brother."

X said to me, "So you don't know anything, or you just can't speak on it?"

"I told you already, I'm waiting to find out just like everybody else," I answered.

Then Preston came running up the stairs and broke the news. "Marcus got arrested for robbery," he said. "And somebody got shot."

"Shiiit," kids said all at once.

"Now don't tell me you weren't close enough to hear that gun go pop," X barked at me.

"Yo, X," Moses jumped in. "Back off, before we find

out what we don't want to know. He opens his mouth here and the DA will try to squeeze us all on the witness stand."

I went straight down the stairs with my blood boiling. And by the time I made it out of the building, the sweat was pouring off of me.

When I got home, Rose was crying. She had called Marcus's house and found out that his mother was on her way to New Jersey. She had no idea why. Neither did I. Casey had given everybody on the team his home number in case of an emergency. But I didn't want to call. And I didn't tell Rose that I had the number, or she would have made me pick up the phone.

I made it through the whole next day at school with my head down. Casey was there for practice, and everyone wanted to talk to him about Marcus. But he wouldn't open his mouth. He just pointed to the locker room for us to change. When we came back out, he was standing on the court with a whistle in his mouth for us to run drills.

We were running an easy layup line, until Casey popped his whistle twice for us to move double-time. Then he crossed both fists over his head. That was the signal for our full court press. The team ran into position on offense and defense. Without Marcus, we had ten players even. So everyone was on the court.

Casey called out the numbers for our set plays. We went through them all, one by one. We ran 5XL for big Andre, 17X for X, and 10C for Moses. I had a bunch of plays that all started with 11, because that was my number. Casey ran them all in a row for me. The last one was 11BW, and Preston took Marcus's place setting the pick on my man that got me free.

Everyone was going hard, like it was for real. We ran every play except for the ones that started with 12. Those belonged to Marcus. When we ran out of plays, Casey blew the whistle and called us over to the bleachers. He lifted the cap off his head, and his face got even more serious.

"I know it's all over school about Marcus. He should be home in the next day or two. When he comes back, give him some room to breathe. Let him concentrate on school and what's ahead of him," Casey said.

Then Casey made sure to look around at everyone and said, "Don't be surprised if the police show up asking questions. I understand they're looking for at least one other person."

I just stared straight ahead.

"Eddie," Casey said. "Do you want to announce your college plans to the team?"

I told them that I had decided on St. John's. I thanked them all for helping me get there, and Casey, too. But when I finished, there wasn't any clapping or congratulations. There was just the sound of the air vents running through the gym.

"You worked hard for that scholarship," Casey said. "You deserve it."

Then he told us all to shower and go home.

I saw Casey sitting in his office before I left. He waved me in with one finger.

"I was hoping to hear about your plans from you, not from St. John's," he said.

"Your right. I'm sorry, Coach," I said. "I've had a lot on my mind since Marcus got locked up. I just haven't been thinking straight."

 BLACK

The cops put me through the system. They took my picture from every side and fingerprinted me. I stayed awake all night in a cell with a bunch of crackheads, afraid to close my eyes on them. There was one toilet in the corner, and everybody could watch you shit and piss. The next morning they shipped me off to the courthouse on Queens Boulevard to see the judge.

I spent most of the day in the pens with a hundred other guys, trying to hold my ground. I had to put on my best ice-grill just to get a little bit of space. Some herb got ripped off for his hooded sweatshirt. And if the officers there didn't put a stop to it, he probably would have went out to see the judge in his under-wear.

I was scared. But I wouldn't show it, or else I would have been shark bait, no matter how big I was.

I was wearing my new kicks from the basketball game, and lots of guys were eyeing them. "He's got

the new Nike joints, and they're just my size," somebody said.

Those damn shoes got me into this mess. But I
wasn't giving anything up to a bunch of thugs. So I
stood up the whole time, with all my weight planted
on top of them.

My stomach was starting to make noise. I hadn't
eaten since lunch at school, the day before. When
they handed out bologna sandwiches with contain-
ers of milk, I wolfed it down like I was eating at Red
Lobster. Other guys with full bellies wouldn't touch
it. And by the time I left to see the judge, the floor was
covered with pink bologna.

They took me into the courtroom, and I saw my
mother sitting with Casey and his wife. It meant
something to me that Coach was there for my mother. I didn't hold it against Eddie for not showing. It
would have been the same as giving himself up. But
right or wrong, I couldn't stop thinking how Eddie
was getting a free ride.

My mother came up and hugged me tight. I could
see in her eyes how she would have liked to break
me in half. I met the lawyer the city appointed to my
case, Ms. Torres. She was talking to my mother
before I came out. So my mother knew about everything I did. Ms. Torres told me what to expect, and

asked if I would identify the shooter to get less time.

I told her no, flat out.

That's when my mother went off, "That's why Eddie's not here! Ain't that right, Marcus! Oh, but he's your best friend in the world. So he'll let you go to jail without him. You just think about—"

She caught herself in one quick breath, and held the rest back. Then her face turned more serious than I'd ever seen it before. She opened her eyes wide and said, "Marcus, I want to know right now if you've got a gun hidden somewhere in that house. I don't want your sister to find it and blow her head off!"

I never thought I'd hear her ask me a question like that.

"No, Mama," I said in a low voice.

Ms. Torres just shook her head.

The clerk called my name and it echoed off all four walls. I felt ashamed that my mother had to hear it. The DA came on and said his piece against me. Ms. Torres just listened and took notes on a long yellow pad. The judge said there was enough evidence to hold me, and set my bail at $20,000. I knew my mother couldn't afford anything close to that. So when it was over, an officer took me back to the pens. And I got put on the next bus to Rikers Island.

I was chained to the kid sitting next to me by the

wrist and leg. There were thick metal screens on the windows, and the driver was separated from us by a steel cage. The bus turned off the highway, and rolled down the side streets, maybe two miles from my house. Then it started over the Rikers Island Bridge.

There was nothing outside the window, except water and razor-wire fences.

Adolescents have their own houses, so the adults can't take advantage of them. I got sent to Mod #1 with all the other newjacks. That's where they keep you until you learn the system on Rikers. But the main part of what goes on there started to sink in right away. It's black people, wall to wall. There are some Spanish inmates, too. But everybody else is black.

That whole first night, I kept thinking how if Eddie got arrested with me, his family would have bailed him out. Only I'd still be there. I couldn't beef about it. It wouldn't have been Eddie's fault. That's the way it is. We could be Black and White anywhere else in the world. But not on Rikers Island.

I saw plenty of white dudes in court. I guess they were innocent, or made bail. The only white faces I saw on Rikers belonged to the corrections officers.

There weren't any cells with iron bars, like in the

movies. Instead, there were rows of cots in a big dorm. I slept in all my clothes that night, with my head under the blanket.

I spent most of the next day feeling my way around. A woman CO put a scrub brush in my hand. I was part of a crew that cleaned the bathroom until it shined. If my mother ever made me to do that, I would have blown. But there I was, cleaning the city's toilets, without making a peep about it.

To get to the mess hall, the officers took us down the main corridor. It's long and narrow, with low a ceiling. The different houses move back and forth on opposite sides, only five or six feet apart. The COs play the middle in between them.

Every time another house passed next to us, kids got tense, like something might jump off. I saw lots of dudes with fresh cuts on their faces, long buck-fifties from ear to jaw that would take more than a hundred stitches to close. And I didn't want to become one of them.

The COs put us at a table in the middle of the mess hall. The houses all around knew we were new-jacks, and kept barking at us. Especially the adults. Most of those dudes were diesel, and could have probably snapped me in half. I heard plenty of shit about taking my sneakers. But I just kept eating, like I was deaf.

On the way back, the house got stopped at the metal detector. Everybody was patted down. A CO wearing rubber gloves ran his hands down my sides and through my pockets. Some kid had snuck out a container of milk. And after the CO found it, he slapped him hard in the back of the head until the kid almost cried.

In the house, I was mostly able to hold my own. It was like summer camp for scumbags. Kids spent all day trying to prove they were gangsters. The sneak thieves stole shit. The maytags had to wash other kids' socks and drawers. The doldiers were muscle for the gangsters, and the thugs did their own fighting. But everyone was scared of being shipped upstate, and doing real time with adults.

The kids that were ready to cop out looked the most shook. They said the adults upstate didn't play bullshit games. They played for keeps. And you'd have to fight to keep from being somebody's boy.

It got to me, too, and I didn't want to think about doing years up there.

At around five o'clock, a CO called me to the front of the house. I was shocked when he told me I was going home on a bail-out. I wanted to be off Rikers Island more than anything. But I didn't know how I was going to face my mother at home.

An officer took me down to the front gate with my paperwork. My mother and sister were waiting just outside the last checkpoint. It looked like the gates at a subway station, with two COs keeping watch. I pushed the bar on the turnstile and felt it come back around and bump me from behind.

Sabrina ran up and hugged me. My mother was waiting with her arms folded across her chest.

"I brought her along because I want her to see what this place is," my mother said before she kissed me on the forehead, without ever opening her arms.

We had to take the 101-Limited over the Rikers Island Bridge, past our house to Queensboro Plaza. Then we took the 19-A back home from there. My mother walked in tight behind me, like they weren't going to let me on that bus anymore because of what I did. But the driver never said a word.

My mother begged her sisters in New Jersey to put up their house for my bail. They hadn't seen me since I was small. So I knew they did it mainly for her, and not me.

There wasn't much talk, except for Sabrina. I kept

my mouth shut and eyes down for most of the ride. I saw every crack in the sidewalk and every piece of trash on the floor of those buses.

Moses and X were hanging out right outside my building. They both gave me a pound, with my mother watching close.

"No matter what, they still got to prove their case against you," X said. "And they get it wrong a lot, brother."

Moses said how much the team missed me in the second half. Then he gave X a sideways look and said, "Your best friend took a scholarship to St. John's before he left the gym that night."

They waited for me to blink. And I won't front—it hurt like anything to hear. But I had bigger things to worry about. So I brushed it off.

My mother heard every word. She was so steamed at Eddie, you could have fried an egg on her forehead. But she didn't blow, either.

We got into the elevator, and the metal door sprung closed behind us. My sister had to jump up a little to hit the top button. We started up, and I could feel the pressure pushing down on me. It felt like my heart was sinking into my shoes.

My mother put the key in our door and opened the

locks one by one. I was never so glad to be home in all my life. But another part of me knew what I was in for that night. And I would have rather been caught stealing money out of my mother's purse than tell her everything I had done.

Sabrina turned on the TV. But my mother shut it back off inside the first minute. She told my sister to study her math and clean up for dinner. There was a knock at the door. My mother shot me a hard look. So I didn't even think about moving. She opened the door without even asking, "Who is it?"

Mrs. Johnson from downstairs was standing there with a pot of stew. She used to be my babysitter. Now she stayed with Sabrina when my mother got outside sewing jobs. They stood at the door and talked about me like I wasn't even there.

"So how is he?" she asked.

"He's still on this earth, if that's what you mean!" my mother answered.

Mrs. Johnson almost laughed and said, "Hold on to that kind of thinking, honey. It'll help you get through this."

That stew was the only real food I had in almost two days. But I didn't enjoy a bite. It was almost eight o'clock when we finished. I carried the dishes to the sink and started to wash them. Then my mother told Sabrina to go to bed early, and went to talk to her.

I heard my mother's footsteps starting back, and I scrubbed the dishes even harder. She pulled the chair out and sat down at the table behind me. I didn't want to turn around for anything. I kept at the dishes until they were whiter than they'd ever been.

"That's enough of that. Come over here and sit down," my mother said.

Her eyes were more sad than angry. We looked at each other for almost a minute without saying a word.

"Explain yourself to me, Marcus!" she finally said, her voice shaking.

Before the first word came out of my mouth, I broke down crying. I looked up and she was crying, too.

"I just wanted some extra money, Mama. I wanted to do things. I wanted to buy these shoes and pay the senior dues, too. I didn't mean for anybody to—"

"You almost killed somebody! Do you understand that? You threw away your life for some spending money and a pair of shoes. And you almost killed a man!" she said. "Now, did I raise you up, or did the streets?" she kept on through the tears.

She asked me why I wouldn't say Eddie's name. She knew he was there with me, and must have had the gun.

"Maybe you won't say his name to the police, but you'll say it here. I don't want to hear any more of this *I* business, because I know it was *we*. It's Black and White until somebody's ass is on the line. And when it's time to go to jail, it's just Black. He'll find a new boy to carry his bags in college, and you'll be an ex-con on the unemployment line!" she screamed.

Sabrina came out of the bedroom crying from all the yelling. My mother held her tight, and buried Sabrina's face in her chest. "I love my babies," she said, rocking her. "Lord knows, I love my babies."

After everything got said out loud, I went to my bed. I thought about Eddie, and what my mother said.

If Eddie had got bagged without me, I don't know how I'd have been acting. I just know I would have been keeping a low profile, too. You don't give your best friend up to the cops. No how. No way. I knew that Eddie would have played it the same way for me.

But that part about the scholarship was sticking in me.

The phone rang. It was like someone sent an electric shock through me. I was sitting up in my bed before the second ring. That's when my mother answered.

"Yes, he's home. But he's asleep now. It's been a long couple of days," she said.

Then she asked, "How's your brother taking all this?"

And I knew it was Rose calling.

"No, I can't talk to him right now, dear. But you let your brother know for me that God has a way of watching over things. Yes, you, too. Good night," she said, and I heard her put the phone down into the cradle.

The next morning, my mother was standing over me, poking my shoulder to get up. She was sending me to school. I took a shower and got dressed. There was oatmeal on the kitchen table, but no place set for me.

"You're going to start doing things for yourself more. Get a bowl and a spoon," she told me.

When I was finished, I went to scrape the last of the oatmeal into the garbage. My new sneakers were sitting right on top, covered in table scraps. The smell came up and hit me good. I just froze there for a second, sick to my stomach. I pushed what was left in my bowl right on top of them, and closed the lid down tight.

I kissed my mother before I left for school. She stood there like a stone statue. When my lips were on her cheek, I could feel everything warm inside her.

But once they came off, she was cold as anything to me again.

I turned the corner outside my building and thought about what I should do. I took two or three steps towards school. Then I stopped. I spun around quick and felt enough momentum to keep going towards Eddie's.

I waited across the street, at the end of the block, behind a thick tree. There were shadows moving inside the house. Rose walked out with her arms folded around a notebook. I called her name the second she stepped outside the gate. Her mouth opened wide. But I put a finger over my lips for her not to make a sound. She looked back towards the house. Then she ran over to me.

Rose said my name and hugged me at the same time. Then she told me what everyone was saying I got arrested for.

"You didn't do any of that, Marcus? Did you?" she asked.

I told her it was an accident that the man got shot. But I could see in her brown eyes how disappointed she was in me.

Rose wanted to know why I didn't just come to the door. I asked her what her mother and father thought about me getting locked up. She dropped her shoulders and said they were both down on me. That's when Eddie stepped outside.

He stood there looking at us while he put the other arm through his coat. I never saw Eddie walk with his arms so stiff. But he put both of them around me before I could lift mine to hug him back.

I told him I'd heard about the scholarship. He said that wasn't important. That we'd both be playing in college soon. Maybe even together.

I didn't believe that. And it didn't sound like Eddie did, either.

Then Eddie asked me about court, and I just held on to myself tight. Part of me wanted to spark off about what I was facing alone now. But I couldn't go there in front of Rose.

"How stressed is your mother?" Eddie asked.

I looked over Rose's head, and caught Eddie's eye.

"She's all over *everything* in this," I said, and watched his face drop straight off.

Then Rose asked how I could get talked into something like that. She said how it wasn't right that whoever did the shooting was off the hook, and that I had to pay for it all. I fought hard to keep my voice even.

"That's just the way the game gets played out," I

said. "The cops do the chasing. It's all about who they catch."

The school block came up fast. We took our ID cards out and passed through security. Two of the school safety officers, Jefferson and Connelly, were at the front desk. They worked security together at all our home games. Kids called them "Black and White wannabes." But they always just smiled at that, and did their jobs.

Jefferson was tall and lean. He played football and basketball when he was a high school kid in Brooklyn. Connelly was almost a head shorter, and weighed close to three hundred pounds. His nose was pushed flat, like a pig's. And if you ever ranked on him about it, he'd make sure you got suspended the same day. He could be all right, but he had a mean streak in him, too.

One day, Connelly went out and bought a brand-new basketball and football for Eddie and me to sign. We knew he wanted them just to sell one day. But that didn't matter. Those were our first autographs.

Connelly took the ID out of my hand. He looked at it like he'd never seen me before. Then he turned to Jefferson and asked, "Do you want to buy half a basketball cheap?" Jefferson didn't crack a smile at that or anything. But when I passed through, Jefferson tapped me on the shoulder, and said he wanted to talk to me about everything later.

When we got out of range, Eddie called Connelly an asshole, and Rose backed him up on it. Deep down, that made me feel better.

Eddie's class was on the first floor. Mine was on the third, the same as Rose's. Halfway up the stairs, Rose said, "I know the two of you keep that game face on all the time, and pretend it's all okay. But I can't even imagine what you're feeling, Marcus. It's been tough on Eddie, too, worrying about you. I heard him crying in his room. It must be a hundred times worse for you."

All morning, kids wanted to know what happened. I just played it cool, and told them that I couldn't talk until everything got straightened out in court. They figured I must have been innocent. Everybody knew I had it going on playing ball. They couldn't see me throwing it all away on a lousy stickup.

I was copying the English notes I'd missed when Eddie walked through the door. His face wasn't showing much of anything. He nodded his head to me. Then Ms. Sussman started her lesson, and Eddie turned back around. He didn't take his eyes off her for the rest of the period.

When the bell rang, Eddie pulled his books together one at a time. He stood up and waited for me. "Coach will probably run us like dogs today with that game on Tuesday," he said.

I would have done anything to hear what was really inside his head. Even if I had to punch him in the jaw to get it out. I pushed my toes into the floor and said, "I wasn't even thinking about that right now."

I went out the door first, with Eddie right behind me. Before I knew it, I was headed to my next class alone.

Later on, I ran into Eddie's mother in front of the cafeteria.

"Rose told me you were here this morning," she said. "I just want you to know that if you can't talk at home, you can come by our house and say anything that's on your mind. Marcus, I want you to know that we're always going to be there for you."

I looked into her eyes and knew how bad she'd feel if she ever found out about Eddie.

"Thanks, but I'll get by all right," I told her.

The noise inside the cafeteria hit me like a wave. Moses and X found me sitting by myself. They were all over me for pulling a stickup on somebody who could point me out so easy. Then they pounded me about messing up my shot at playing college ball.

"So the dude didn't remember what your partner, Al Capone, looked like?" asked Moses.

"Of course not," cracked X. "He was so shocked the black kid wasn't the one holding the gun, he couldn't take his eyes off Marcus."

No matter how bad they got on my case, at least it was real.

"You don't have a paid lawyer. You don't have a co-defendant to take half the blame. You're fucked!" X said.

"The only thing in your favor is the dude who got shot is black. Maybe the judge won't give a damn, unless the judge is black, too," said Moses.

All through math class, I only saw the back of Eddie's head. The teacher gave a pop quiz. I ran through it easy because they were questions we had from the beginning of the year. I could see Eddie was stuck on the last problem. I thought about kicking his chair twice for the letter "B." But my leg wouldn't move.

We walked upstairs to practice together, and started to change. The last time I was in that locker room the cops were handcuffing me. Now I didn't have anything to hide, except for Eddie's part.

Eddie saw me lacing up my old kicks and asked about my sneakers.

"My mother chucked the new ones in the garbage," I told him.

He stood there looking at me, until his eyes dropped down to his own shoes.

Coach was all over everybody at practice for making little mistakes or not hustling. I only screwed up one time. But when I did, Casey jumped on me, too. It felt good to take the heat for something small again, like screwing up on a basketball court.

After I caught my first wind, I fell right in step. The ball was moving back and forth between Eddie and me like nothing ever came between us. We had guys flying in every direction. No one could read our moves. And every time they tried to double-team one of us, the ball got passed quick to whoever was open.

I blocked everything else out of my mind and just played ball.

When Casey blew the last whistle, I was drenched in sweat. I didn't want to towel off. I wanted to keep playing. Eddie and everybody else went in to change, but I just kept shooting the ball by myself. It was the first time I could remember that Casey didn't give his Friday speech about keeping out of trouble over the weekend.

By the time I went inside, Eddie was already dressed. So I threw sweats and a jacket on over what I was wearing. Neither one of us said a word until we got down the stairs and the door to the school slammed shut behind us.

We were at the first corner waiting for the light to change when Eddie asked, "Is there something I'm supposed to do?"

"There's nothing to do," I came back. "That man recognized me, and now I got to deal with it."

"How rough was it?" Eddie asked.

I told Eddie the cops had me sewed up tight from the beginning. But I wouldn't tell them anything more. Then Eddie said he dumped the gun where nobody would ever find it. He didn't say where, and I didn't ask.

I told Eddie how my mother knew from the start it was him with the gun. But I didn't think I could get across how mad she was. So I didn't even try.

"You know I only took that scholarship right away in case they started to hear things later," he said.

"When shit jumps up, I guess you got to move fast," I said. "I'll be playing somewhere, too, after the judge and my mother finish kicking my ass."

We stopped a few blocks before our houses. I asked Eddie if he was worried about being seen with me in the streets. That the cops might figure it out for themselves.

He thought about it for a few seconds and said, "Who doesn't already know about Black and White?"

We both smiled at that, and went home our separate ways.

WHITE

I saw the black sedan parked outside of my house. Right away, I knew that something was wrong. There were two open spots on either side. But the car was parked in front of the hydrant anyway. I could hear my dad's voice from inside. It was loud and polite, like he was talking to company. I turned the knob and everything inside got quiet.

Two detectives were sitting on the couch, facing me. One of them stood up and stretched out his long legs. The other one stayed where he was, and said, "This must be your son, Eddie."

My mom came over and put both her hands around my shoulders. She steered me through the living room like I was blind and she had just changed all the furniture around.

The one who was standing took a giant step towards me and stuck out his hand. "I'm Detective Smoltz," he said, as my fingers disappeared inside his grip. He squeezed my hand and looked straight into my eyes. It felt like he could pull anything he wanted right out of me. From across the room, my dad was staring me in the face. I thought he was about to scream at me. Then his eyes bounced between the two detectives, and he got himself together.

Gotti was anchored at the feet of the one sitting down. The detective got up only halfway, and leaned forward. He stayed low enough to keep petting Gotti with one hand, while he shook mine with the other. "Eddie, my name is Detective O'Grady," he said. "My partner and I want to talk to you about a string of robberies and a shooting."

O'Grady asked a lot of questions about Marcus. My mom and dad answered a couple of them before I could even open my mouth. He knew all about Black and White, and my scholarship to St. John's. He asked what me and Marcus liked to do after practice. That's when my dad got really upset, and wanted to know if they were investigating me.

"We're just trying to understand what happened that night," O'Grady said. "We know that Eddie spends a lot of time with Marcus. Maybe he can be helpful."

Rose came home right behind me, and my mom tried to take her upstairs. But she wanted to tell the detectives how nice Marcus treated everybody. She said that if Marcus had done something bad, that it was probably because somebody talked him into it. That he was still part of our family, no matter what.

Then Smoltz asked, "Do you folks keep a .38 caliber revolver in this house?"

My mom and Rose let out a gasp that sent Gotti into a barking fit. "We don't own a gun!" my dad said in a charged-up voice. Then he made a speech about how we were a taxpaying family, and that there were real criminals running around the streets. Through that whole scene, Smoltz and O'Grady never took their eyes off of me.

I didn't know where to put my hands or how to hold my arms. The detectives on TV were experts at reading body language, so I figured that they probably were, too. I went over and stood between my mom and Rose, and they both wrapped their arms around me. Now they'd have to judge me between two people who had nothing to hide.

Before they left, O'Grady gave me his card and said, "Call me if you remember something that can make it easier on Marcus. No one wants to see him get what he doesn't deserve."

The door closed behind them and I didn't know what to do next. My dad started ripping into Marcus. Rose and my mom were yelling at him to stop.

"It's where he was brought up," he said. "It's either

rob or be robbed. But everybody here goes around saying he's part of this family. Now the police are at our door."

Rose wanted to call Marcus to tell him about the detectives. But my parents wouldn't let her, and told me not to call, either. They said that we should keep some distance until the investigation was finished. My mom was so upset that she couldn't make dinner. And things didn't settle down until she sent my dad out for Chinese food.

I sat down on the couch in the spot where O'Grady had been sitting. It was still warm. I wasn't about to give the cops anything to work with. But no matter how I explained it to myself, I couldn't get away from how I was turning my back on Marcus. It wasn't Black and White anymore. It was just me looking out for my own ass.

I held O'Grady's card in front of my face. I looked at all the numbers and the police department seal up in the corner. I felt everything I ever worked for slipping away—my scholarship, the pros—everything.

I knew that the cops figured out it was me with Marcus that night. They probably just didn't have enough evidence to prove it, or they would have arrested me. I folded the card in half and buried it in my pocket.

That night I couldn't sleep. I heard the floor in the attic creak. I got out of bed. I knew I had to face what was up there. I could see a light from under the door as I got closer. When I got to the top of the steps, I pushed the door open.

My dad was staring right at me. He was sitting on grandpa's bed with the shoe box in his hands. The rubber bands were still wrapped around it. I stood in the doorway, waiting for him to say something. He weighed the box in his palm and shook it to hear the sound it made.

"I don't ever want to open this box, Eddie. Do I?" he asked.

I looked him in the eye as long as I could.

He never raised his voice. He just told me to get my ass back in bed. And I did. I don't know what he did with the box after that, but in the morning it was gone. He didn't tell my mom a thing about it, either. He acted like it never happened. Only I could see it behind his eyes, no matter how hard he tried to hide it. It was a look that said, "How could I raise you to do something like that?" And when my mom mentioned Marcus that morning, I saw the explosion inside of him.

I spent that whole Saturday trying to stay out of his sight. I didn't want to go to the Circle and run into Marcus, either. So I shot fouls for almost two hours on the courts over by the D.S. In all the time I was there, maybe twenty sanitation trucks rolled in and out of the big garage. The crews on more than half of them stopped to congratulate me on getting the scholarship. Dad had bragged to everyone he worked with. Now he was at home, pretending that he was still proud of me.

On Sunday morning at eleven o'clock, O'Grady and Smoltz showed up. They shook my dad's hand at the front door and wiped their feet on the welcome mat. Then they arrested me in my living room. My mom and Rose were at church. I was glad they weren't around to see it. Gotti growled at the detectives and showed them his teeth. So my dad had to drag him out to the backyard.

O'Grady said that the woman who had been robbed picked my picture out of the school yearbook. Smoltz went upstairs to search my room. But he came back shaking his head. They took me out onto the front porch in handcuffs. Some of the neighbors were even outside. My dad was walking right behind us. I wouldn't turn around to look at him.

"Don't say anything until I get you a lawyer," I heard him say from over my shoulder.

O'Grady pushed my head down as he put me into the backseat of the car. I could hear Gotti barking from around back until O'Grady slammed the door shut. Then they took me away, with my dad watching from the curb.

At the station house, they asked me questions for almost two hours. But I wouldn't say a word. Keeping my mouth shut and waiting for a lawyer was tough. But listening to how they had it all pieced together was even harder. Smoltz liked telling it again and again, and watching me sweat. They knew about everything, except for my grandpa's gun.

"Sooner or later, Marcus is going to fill in all the cracks for us. His lawyer will wise him up. You'll see," said O'Grady. "That will leave you holding the gun, Eddie. That's just the way it works. Time is time. There is no more Black and White. Those days are over. Nobody is going to watch your back anymore but you."

Smoltz explained how I could come clean, and maybe the DA would agree to go easier on me. Then he explained how Marcus could get that same deal for himself, and stick it to me.

"My partner and I have been together for nine years," O'Grady said. "What would you do if I shot somebody and asked you to keep it quiet, Detective Smoltz?"

"I'd turn you over in a heartbeat," answered Smoltz.

I spent the night in central booking, and everything they said started echoing in my ears. I didn't get a wink of sleep. All the thugs and drunks in the cell were acting up. But I would have fought every one of them, and kicked their asses, too, if it could erase everything I did.

The next morning, I got transferred to the court-house by bus. In the pens, I had my game face on. I heard lots of talk about me being a "white boy."

The system wasn't hard to figure out. You went into the courtroom, and unless someone knew your face from *America's Most Wanted*, the judge gave you bail. But lots of guys couldn't pay it. They came back to the pens bitching, and the guards put them on the bus for Rikers Island.

I got called out to a side room to meet my lawyer, Mr. Golub. My dad found him through his boss, whose son had fucked up once, too. He explained to me what would happen out in the courtroom, and what I should say. Then he would meet with me and my dad in a few days, after he studied the case more.

When I got back to the pens, I caught an earful.

"Tell me a white boy came back from seeing the judge and is going to the Island," one guy said.

"Get real now. Money came back from talking with his mouthpiece. That's all!" said another black dude.

I stood up in front, against the bars. That's where the officers had their desk.

"Big boy, you feel safer up here?" one of the offi-cers grinned.

I thought about how it was different when me and

Marcus had each other's backs. I knew that I was going home in a couple of hours. Then I'd only have to worry about my mom, and what the coach at St. John's would say.

There were two other white guys who got called out ahead of me. Neither one of them came back. That didn't bother me.

An officer walked me into the courtroom, and we came out from behind the flag. Mom and Rose were sitting in the first row, sharing rosary beads. Their eyes were red and swollen from crying. My dad looked me up and down, like he hardly knew me.

The DA read the evidence against me out loud, and my mom let out a sob. My lawyer said something in legal talk. Then the judge asked me if I understood everything. "Yes, sir," I answered.

I couldn't believe this was happening. But it was.

There was some more talk between the lawyers and the judge. When it was over, I had bail.

BLACK

Rose called my house on Sunday night. My mother picked up the phone, and only let me talk to her because she was so hysterical. I tried my best to talk her down. But she just kept asking, "Is it true, Marcus? Is it true?"

I kept sidestepping her, saying that Eddie would be all right. That he could handle it, and he'd probably be home by the next day. But I wasn't about to put Eddie in that car with me. Not to anyone. Especially Rose.

She said she was outside at a pay phone, so her parents wouldn't know she was calling. My mother was right next to me, listening to every word out of my mouth. When I hung up the phone, she said, "I don't wish anything on the family of those who do wrong. Lord knows, I've had to deal with that myself. But now that boy knows what it's like to be locked up, too."

My mother laid it down right. Eddie was as guilty as me. Maybe even a little more. She spent the rest of the night humming a church hymn. I remember lying in bed, staring up at the dark ceiling with the sound of it echoing through the house.

The next morning at school, Officer Jefferson pulled me aside, with Connelly smirking from behind his desk. He put a hand on my shoulder and started up the stairs with me. Jefferson worked all our home games and rooted for us hard. He knew that my father wasn't around anymore, so he cheered extra loud for me. It made me feel like somebody from my family was always at the game. I had a lot of respect for him. He put that uniform on every day, and did his best with kids. When there was drama in the halls, he'd put himself right in the middle of it. I never saw him take the easy way out once. When two black kids went at it, he'd get them both together when it was over with. He'd explain how black people had enough trouble in this world without them going at each other. So I knew what was coming. And when I didn't deny my part in the stickup, Jefferson let me have it with both barrels.

"I don't know if it was your bad idea, or somebody with even less sense talked you into it, son. But it was wrong. Just plain wrong," Jefferson started out. "If they send you upstate, you'll have real, everyday time to think about it. Time when there's nothing else between you and what you did. But I want to know what gives you the right to pull a gun on someone, especially another black man? Do you want a part in putting more fatherless black children on the street? Don't you know enough of them already?" he asked, without raising his voice for anyone else to hear.

Everything he said hit deep, and I wanted to take off running from underneath his arm. But I stayed there and took it, because I knew he was right. And I promised him I'd never be that stupid in my life again.

At practice, everybody was asking me about Eddie. It was the first time in almost four years he wasn't there. Casey raised his eyebrows, but he never said a word to me about it. Our final game of the regular season was the next day at Hillcrest High School in Jamaica, Queens. Missing practice before a game meant Eddie couldn't start. But he had more to worry about than that now.

After practice, guys were ripping Eddie for being AWOL right after getting his scholarship. I listened to it all without opening my mouth. Then Casey came in and announced that Preston would be starting the next day. Kids howled at a freshman taking Eddie's spot, and couldn't wait to see the look on his face. None of them really cared. It was a throwaway game for us before the playoffs started the next week. Only Casey was really pissed off at Eddie.

That night, I picked up a basketball and told my mother I had to blow off some steam, or else I'd bust wide open. Her face turned rock-hard. But she didn't say anything to stop me.

I dribbled right through the courts in the Circle, and headed straight for Eddie's house. The lights were on in the living room with the drapes halfway open. I walked past and tried to peek inside. Eddie's father was sitting on the sofa, talking to someone. But that was all I could see. So I walked around the block to make another pass.

The next time around, I stopped in front of the window and bent down even with the top of the gate. A car in the street honked its horn, and I almost jumped out of my skin. That's when I saw Eddie walk through the living room. I stood back up quick, and got out of there.

The next morning, I saw Rose in the hallway up ahead of me at school. She was walking in my direction, until she turned inside a classroom. It was crowded in the hall, and I couldn't tell for sure if she saw me. Rose had never ditched me before. I thought about her over the next two periods, and it just ate at me.

Eddie was standing outside the door to English, talking to Rebecca. He saw me coming and kissed her good-bye on the lips. I could see by the way his mouth was curled up that he wanted to be the first one to say something.

"Nobody else knows, and that's the way I want to keep it," he whispered to me.

I just nodded my head, and asked if he was all right.

"My lawyer says we'll both be all right if we keep our mouths shut," he came back.

Eddie said that he had to come to school, or he wouldn't be able to play at all in the game that day. Then St. John's would see his name missing from the box score, and would want to know what happened.

Ms. Sussman stuck her head into the hallway and told us to come in for class. She called us "gentlemen." So Eddie put his arm out in front of him, and bowed to her before we went inside.

All through class, Eddie had his notebook open and the point of his pen on the paper. But that was just to keep Ms. Sussman off his back. He spent most of the time glued to whatever business was rolling around in his head.

When the bell finally rang, Eddie waited for me at his desk.

"What did Coach say about me missing practice?" he asked.

I told him that Preston was starting in his place. But Eddie didn't even blink over the news.

"No way I'm getting on that bus today," he said. "We're going to make sure that everybody walks over to the train."

I hadn't even thought about it. The whole team usually hopped the bus outside of school and took it down to the subway station. The only other way was to walk the five or six blocks over to the N train, and make the next connection from there. I just knew that I didn't want to get on that bus, either.

Eddie's mother was working the cafeteria door. I didn't want to face her for anything. So I skipped lunch and headed for the library. I sat down by myself at one end of a long table.

A kid at the next table over was reading *The Count of Monte Cristo*. There was a drawing on the cover of the two ex-friends fighting each other. That was Eddie's favorite part from the movie. I tried to picture his face on one of the characters. I could see Eddie's hands and feet moving fast, and hear the swords hitting against each other. Then the flash of a red jacket went past. I looked up and it was Rose.

She stopped short when she saw me. I followed her eyes from where she was looking down at me, and swallowed hard.

Rose pulled out a chair and parked herself across from me. Her mouth opened wide like a storm of words was about to come roaring out. But she choked it all back. She took a quick breath and pushed her elbows into the table.

"How did it ever get like this?" she whispered in a strained voice.

I reached over and put my hand on top of hers. "It's mostly my fault," I said. "I let everybody down. I just—"

That's when the librarian leaned in over my shoulder. She took her glasses off and let them hang down from a string of glass beads around her neck. She cleared her throat and said, "This is not an appropriate place to hold a conversation. Can you please have some consideration for everyone else here?"

She was looking straight at me, but I couldn't tell

if she was waiting for an answer or not. So I played it safe and just kept nodding my head until she finally left.

Rose slipped her hand out from mine. She was losing it. Her fingers were pressed up against her eyes to stop the tears. Then the bell rang, and all I could hear was the sound of books being slammed shut.

WHITE

I showed my math teacher the early excuse note. Then I headed upstairs to the gym. Marcus and most of the other guys were already outside of Casey's office.

"Yo, college star, did you bring your long underwear today? I hear it can get really cold warming the bench," snapped X.

Everybody was laughing. So I put a smile on my face and sucked it up.

"Are you just too important to practice with us now, White?" asked Big Andre.

I started to answer, but Casey's door popped open and everybody turned back around.

Casey looked us over to see who was there. And I dropped my head before his eyes found mine. He reminded us what train stop to get off at, and not to get into any fights with other kids on the way.

"Eddie, what happened to you yesterday?" he asked out of nowhere.

Everybody except for Marcus had their eyes drilled into me.

"I had to be somewhere with my family," I said.

I knew that it sounded more like I had been to a funeral than to jail.

Casey sent us out, and I was the first one to the staircase. Down four flights, footsteps were building up behind me. They were right on my tail as I hit the first floor. Connelly was busy on the phone. He put up a flabby arm to stop me. I pulled up short, and the team piled up at my back. Connelly slammed the receiver down. He took a deep breath and squeezed his fat ass into a chair. Then he counted us, and scribbled the number in his book.

"I'd tell you boys to shoot the lights this afternoon, but that might make me an accessory," he laughed.

"Harr, harr, harr," X barked back at him like a seal. "That's so funny."

Everyone bolted for the front door before Connelly had a chance to jerk us around. On the front steps everybody started barking because they knew that Connelly could still hear us from inside. I joined in, too. It felt great. Then somebody oinked like a pig to really screw with Connelly's head, and everybody else started, too.

The wind had died down, and in the sun, it was

almost warm. Marcus stepped to the front of the pack, oinking louder than anybody. He walked right past the bus stop and started for the train on Broadway. The team just followed along, laughing and making different animal noises like it was feeding time at the Bronx Zoo.

We started out on a platform fifty feet above the street. The train came rolling in and we took over one end of a car. Kids were starting to jaw at me again for missing practice. But the sound of the train muffled most of it out.

At an underground station, we transferred over to the F train. The subway has a different feel to it when it's below ground. Instead of blue sky and white clouds, there's nothing but black outside the windows. The whole mood changes, and you can see that people are more uptight.

At the other end of the car, a man started screaming at a woman and her baby. At first, I thought they were together and just having a fight. Then the man really went off on her. And you could tell that he was crazy.

"Stupid niggers, you're all the same. Go back to the fuckin' jungle," he screamed at the woman, and started over in our direction.

The man had on a short black coat and brown wool

cap. He was tall, and staggering more than he was walking.

"Hitler didn't go far enough, Rabbi," he yelled at some guy with glasses and a beard, wearing a yarmulke. "He should have killed all the niggers, and your Jewish mother, too."

I thought the guy was going to get up and sock him for sure, talking about his mother that way. But he just kept on reading, and never even looked up from his book.

The lunatic was white. But the dirt was so thick on his face that it was hard to tell. He lost his balance and crashed face-first up against the doors. That's when the whole team wanted to puke, and turned their heads away. The back of his pants were brown where the shit stains had come through. Kids were holding their noses, and yelling at him to leave. He didn't want any part of us, so he started in with some white girl, who was sitting alone.

"One day, niggers are going to fuck you, too," he told her, leaning up against the doors. "They're going to fuck you good, and you'll love it!"

I looked over at Marcus, and he was looking right back at me. Other kids were howling. But not us. Maybe a month ago, we'd have been laughing, too. I kept thinking about being locked up with a nut-job like that and having to listen to his act twenty-four/seven. Besides, that could have been my sister sitting there by herself.

The two halves of the door opened at the next station, and someone pushed the man out of the train. Everybody clapped for the guy who did it. But just as the doors closed, that loony stepped back inside. He started up again with the girl, telling her that sooner or later some black guy was going to ramrod her. An old lady got up and tried to move into the next car, but the door was locked.

When the train finally stopped again, the man wandered out onto the platform. Kids had their faces pressed up against the windows, watching him. He was already hassling the people outside. After the doors closed, everyone started banging on the windows, calling him "Shit Drawers." That's when he gave us all the finger with both hands.

We got to Hillcrest before Casey, who had to teach his last class. In the locker room, Preston was trying not to smile too much about starting. But everyone was busy putting a battery in his back, telling him that he was the new "White" in Black and White.

I didn't know how hard to go in the warm-ups. I never had to get loose and sit back down before. Marcus leaned in over my shoulder at the back of the layup line and said, "Coach is just playing it straight. There are rules for everything. And everybody's got to pay some kind of price."

Casey got there about ten minutes before we started. He huddled us up at our bench and said that he wanted to go into the playoffs off of a strong last game in the regular season. Hillcrest had a decent squad, but we beat them by fifteen points at our gym almost a month back. That was right after me and Marcus pulled our first stickup. I went into that game on a real high, and scored close to thirty points. Now I was stuck on the bench with the whole world hanging over my head. The only things I could say I had going for me were the scholarship to St. John's and Marcus keeping quiet.

On the opening tip-off, two kids collided and the ball went rolling free. Marcus tracked it down and found Preston standing alone under the basket for an easy score. Like everybody else on the bench, I clapped for them.

A minute or two into the game, I saw my dad and his boss walk into the gym. They sat down in the second row of the stands, on the other side of the court. My dad kept looking at me, until he knew for sure that I saw him.

All through the first quarter, I kept an eye on the clock ticking down. I was waiting for Casey to call my name. Every time he turned in my direction to follow the play, I thought he was going to put me into the game.

We were ahead 12–10 when the Hillcrest coach called a timeout with 3:22 left in the first quarter. I stood up, while the players from the court grabbed a seat. Everyone circled around Casey. He was talking about how the other team was trapping us in the corners. I couldn't stop looking at the sweat rolling down the faces of Preston and Marcus.

The game started up again. A minute later, Casey dropped a hand on my back, and pushed me towards the scorer's table. I was down on one knee, waiting for a stop in play so I could get onto the court. For more than two minutes of game time, everything ran smooth and the refs didn't blow a single whistle. The ball finally kicked out of bounds with just eight seconds left. Preston ran right past me to the bench, slapping my hand on the way. Hillcrest in-bounded the ball, and I chased my man across the court on defense. The buzzer sounded to end the first quarter. Everything inside of me stopped again.

I missed my first couple of shots to start the second quarter. But Marcus kept working me the ball. I finally found the soft spot in the other team's zone, and got on track. My dad and his boss were clapping and calling out my name every time I scored. I had twelve points by halftime, but we were still behind by two.

In the locker room, Casey threw a fit. He said we were playing like the other team was going to just hand us the game. He challenged everyone to play harder, and come together "as a team." We all went back onto the court breathing fire, and ready to run through a brick wall to win.

All through the second half, Hillcrest had an answer for everything we did. I'd make a tough shot, and somebody on their squad would do the same. We couldn't get a lead bigger than two or three points. The score was tied with just a couple of minutes to go. Then Marcus found Moses cutting wide open to the hoop. He put the rock right on his hands. But Moses couldn't squeeze it, and lost the ball out of bounds. That's when everything went downhill.

We were down by one point with less than a minute to play. Andre had me standing alone on the baseline. I had both hands out in front of me, waiting to shoot the ball the second I got it. But the big man sailed the pass over my head. We didn't score for the rest of the game, and lost by five points.

Casey made us go over and shake hands with the other team. They had a look on their faces like they couldn't believe that they really beat us. I hated that, and just faked shaking hands down the line. Before we went in to change, Casey pulled us all together.

"We let each other down as a team today," Casey said. "It started with Eddie Russo missing practice, and carried over to some stupid mistakes we made on the court. You need trust out there. Trust to give the ball up to the open man. And trust that you'll get it back when you're open. But it was all just selfish today."

I couldn't believe that Casey mentioned me first. Not after some of the bonehead plays our guys made.

My dad was waiting at the edge of the court. When Coach finished with the team, I walked over to him. He said that his boss was going to drive us home. He didn't have to tell me not to invite Marcus.

A woman reporter who covers high school sports for the *Daily News* was talking with Casey. Me and Marcus had been interviewed by her lots of times. I couldn't believe that she was covering a nothing game like this. I knew that she had to ask Casey why I didn't start. I thought that maybe she wanted to talk about me choosing St. John's.

There was another man with her, carrying a pad and pencil, too. Coach called me and Marcus over. The other reporter introduced himself, and said that he covered the city section. All the time, Casey had his arms folded in front of him, and wouldn't budge off that guy's shoulder.

"I understand that Eddie was arrested on Sunday on the same charge as Marcus," the reporter said quietly. "I'd like to ask you both some—"

That's when Casey stopped him. My dad stepped in and pulled me away. His boss told the reporters that they should save any questions for my lawyer.

Dad waited outside the locker room door while I stuffed my street clothes into a gym bag. On my way back out, Marcus and Casey were just coming inside. I slowed up enough to see their faces. Marcus looked like he was doing all right. But Coach was staring straight ahead, and wouldn't even look at me.

B**LACK**

On my way to school the next morning, I got a newspaper. There was a story about Eddie and me being charged with the stickups and shooting. The headline over it read, *"High School Athletes Charged with Dropping the Ball."*

The story told all about how Sidney Parker, a bus driver on the route that ran past my house, had recognized me. It said that he was the father of three children and hoped to be back at work in another month.

The article kept on about what Parker said. "I've never been afraid of young people. I've always been afraid for them. But I'm angry as hell, too. I'm angry these kids think it's all right to do anything to get what they want. I guess some of them deserve to be locked up like animals."

Then Parker told how he nailed me. "I just couldn't look at that gun pointing at me. So I turned my head and was facing the other kid. Then I remembered where I saw him before."

I read his words over and over, until I knew them by heart. I tossed the paper away a block before school. But when I stepped through the front door, Jefferson and Connelly had one opened on their desk. I could see the headline upside down in front of me. Connelly buried his face in it and started reading the article out loud. Jefferson said good morning to me, talking right over his partner's voice.

Eddie didn't come to school that morning. His mother and Rose weren't there, either. In English, Ms. Sussman blew a fuse after some kid passed a newspaper around in the middle of class. When she was done screaming, her eyes started to water up. She went out in the hallway for a few seconds and pulled herself back together fast.

At lunch, Moses and X never stopped talking about my case. They said that Eddie getting charged was the best thing that could happen to me.

"Now you got somebody to take half the heat, and that somebody is white," X said.

"I'll bet Eddie's father's a Mason like most of the judges," Moses said. He'll probably throw up some secret hand signs that only other Masons know. Then the judge will go easy on him. That's got to rub off on you, too."

That sounded crazy to me, but I didn't want to argue over any of it.

X brought up the idea that Eddie might be at the DA's office working out a deal for himself. One that wouldn't cut me any slack at all. But I couldn't buy it. I couldn't believe Eddie would ever play me dirty, not even with the DA breathing down his neck—and maybe even his parents.

After school, I didn't want to go home for any-thing. I knew that someone would have shown my mother the paper, and she'd be steaming. There was never practice the day after a game. The playoffs were starting next Friday, and Casey would push us hard that whole week. But I wanted to feel a basket-ball in my hands, so I headed upstairs to the gym.

The place was empty, except for Casey and some other gym teachers working in their offices. I took the last practice ball from the rack. The one that nobody else ever wanted to use. It was probably ten years old, and the leather grips had worn down to nothing. But it always felt perfect when I spread my fingers around it.

I passed underneath the glass case on the wall

that holds Jason's white home jersey. He wore Number 15, and nobody else is ever allowed to have that number again. I bowed my head out of respect. Then I stepped out onto the court.

I raised up off both feet with the ball high over my head. At the top of my arc, I let the ball roll off my fingertips. My right wrist fell loose into a perfect gooseneck and the ball slipped through the net. I made that same shot over and over. And the deeper I got into a good groove, the more I was sure that Eddie would never stab me in the back.

I had been shooting for maybe twenty minutes when Casey came out. He started feeding me passes, and I buried a half dozen shots. Then he walked the ball out to where I was standing.

"This thing got a lot of attention today," he said. "Coaches are probably going to walk away from the idea of giving you a scholarship. You might have to play at a city college for a while, until you can prove yourself again."

He didn't even mention the idea of me sitting in a prison cell for the next few years. And I was glad not to hear it.

Casey said he had already called my mother. That she had seen the article and was spitting fire over it. He told me that he called Eddie's house, too.

But he only got the answering machine there.

My mother had calmed down by the time I got home. But she was all business that night. She had talked to my lawyer, Ms. Torres, who told her I didn't have many choices. That by the end of the week, a grand jury was going to indict me for sure. That in a trial, there was no way she could make Sidney Parker look like a liar. So unless I wanted to take a big hit, I was going to have to cop a plea. Then the state would go easier on me for saving them money by skipping a trial.

She told my mother I should work on getting letters from my teachers, saying I was a good student. I knew I could count on Coach and Ms. Sussman for that.

A *Daily News* was sitting closed on the kitchen table the whole time my mother was talking. Eddie's name didn't come up once. Then she caught me looking down at the paper.

"What kind of deal is your best friend working out for himself?" she said in a sharp voice. "Or didn't he talk to you about it yet?"

"Look, you don't know what Eddie's doing!" I answered.

"Neither do you!" she said, with a hand out in front of her to slow herself down. "Neither—do—you, Marcus."

"I know we *both* screwed up," I told her. "And you're right: he's my *best* friend!"

"And you're my son," she came back at me. "Who else is going to look after you? The Russos?"

Those words were like the last good shot in a street fight. I didn't open up my mouth again, and neither did my mother. Only she didn't have anything left to prove.

Eddie was back in school the next day. At practice, the rest of the team didn't even mention the story. Casey wouldn't touch it, either, and stuck to basketball. When practice was over, kids gave us so much space in the locker room that we wound up walking out together.

After the first block, we hit a red light and the traffic was too much to cross against. "So I guess a grand jury is going to indict us," I said.

"My lawyer says that the DA could indict a ham sandwich if he wanted to. That's why we don't even have to be there to open our mouths," he answered back, moving out into the street.

Eddie timed the cars just right and ran over to the other side. I was caught flat-footed and just watched him sail across. When I finally reached him, Eddie said, "Besides, the woman who picked out my picture isn't even a hundred percent sure."

He told me that the coach of St. John's called his house and left a message. The coach wanted to know what was going on, and for Eddie and his parents to get back to him. Eddie's father had his lawyer call back instead, saying that Eddie was innocent and would be there in September.

Eddie kept his eyes straight ahead the whole time he was talking. I watched the side of his face pull tight when he called us a team. He said the DA couldn't prove a thing. Not the way he needed to in court. And that the cops were just fishing for one of us to get scared.

I never said a word back to him about it. The only time he turned to look at me was when we split up to go home. He made a fist and put it out in front of him to connect with mine. "When we win the city championship, they'll have to write a bigger story about Black and White," he said.

I had to finish an essay for Ms. Sussman's class that night. Everybody had the same topic: How do you want people to remember you? I wrote that people should remember I was a good person. That I watched out for my family and friends and never bothered anybody. And that I tried my best at everything I ever did. It looked all right on paper, but I kept thinking about the stickups. So I started another essay. I wrote about being remembered for doing more good things than bad. And that I was lucky to have family and friends who cared about me. I put my name at the top of it and chucked the first one into the garbage.

I wasn't going to lunch because I didn't know what to say to Eddie's mother. But the next day, I passed her in the hall. We were on opposite sides of the white line that runs down the middle of the floor. There were lots of kids between us. So all we had to do was turn our heads and keep on walking.

Casey had us working on our fast break at practice. We'd move the ball all the way up the court without taking a single dribble. A kid standing under the basket would pretend to snap down a rebound, slapping the ball between his hands. He'd turn and hit a second kid running at half-court with a pass. In one motion, that player would zip the ball to the third kid streaking up ahead of him, and he'd lay it in. When it all worked out, you could hear the ball pop off kids' hands, one-two-three. You could close your eyes and know if they did it right by the sound.

Coach hadn't made a Friday speech since I got arrested. But before we went in to get changed, he called us over to the bleachers.

"I know it's been a rough couple of weeks for us as

a team," Casey said. "But we're all going to get through this season together. Everybody's going to learn something from it, including me. I just want you to remember, we didn't get to be a team because we're all wearing the same color uniform. We did it by working together and by sticking up for each other. So in the locker room, on the court and in school, stay focused on supporting each other. That's what being a team's all about."

It was a good speech, and some of us even started talking it up before we got back inside to change. Too bad that it had to be about Eddie and me, and not about winning the playoffs.

Eddie was the first to finish getting dressed. He leaned over to me and said he had to meet his father somewhere. He dropped a hand on my back, and he bounced.

Ms. Torres called that night to tell me I had been indicted. She said that if I agreed to cop a plea, she could get me home inside of two years. And that if I would give up the shooter, she could do even better for me. I told her to take the plea. My mother stared me down, and started drumming her fingers on the kitchen table.

WHITE

I studied the diplomas on Golub's office wall. He graduated from St. John's before he went to law school at the University of Connecticut. He talked about the case with my dad, and how he would get me off. The two of them went over all the holes the state had to fill in. The DA didn't have a gun, or a witness who said I was the shooter. Sidney Parker couldn't pick out my picture. And the woman who identified me wasn't positive.

The two of them talked about me like I was completely innocent. It didn't bother me to hear Golub talk that way. He was my lawyer. He was getting paid to believe in me. But I could hear in my dad's voice what he knew about the gun. I hated making a liar out of him, and I knew how angry he was.

"But can we trust Marcus not to claim you were there?" Golub said. "When the noose gets tight around somebody's neck, they're liable to say anything to save their own skin."

"And even if he did, who'd believe him?" my dad sneered.

"We'll worry about that when or if it happens," Golub answered.

On the way home, I thanked my dad for everything he was doing for me. But he just said, "Do you know how much money this is costing me and your mother?"

That night, I was doing sets of push-ups when Rose marched into my room. She said she just couldn't believe that me and Marcus could really do something so crazy.

"How could you point a gun at someone?" she asked.

"I don't know," I answered her, with my stomach flat against the floor.

That was about the biggest confession I had made to anyone.

Rose went on about me and Marcus going to jail, and how it would ruin the rest of our lives. I told her that my lawyer was on top of things. That I'd beat the case and play in college next year.

"If that bus driver wasn't so sure it was Marcus, this wouldn't be happening," I said.

"I guess that would have made everything all right," she said, kicking me in the ass.

On Saturday, it got all the way up to fifty-five degrees, without any wind at all. When it's cold for a long time, any little bit of sun feels like summer. I knew the Circle would be packed with players. By one o'clock, it would be prime time. That's when the older guys, who partied late on Friday night, would get out of bed and fill the courts. Me and Marcus had made every Saturday at the Circle for almost five years straight. We worked our way up from the bottom of the pile to the top. It killed me to think about not playing on a day that nice. But everybody there would be asking me about what happened. Besides, the cops might even be watching the park undercover, trying to show we did everything together.

By two o'clock, I was bored out of my mind and decided to go out. I wore heavy jeans and a pair of Timberlands. That way, no matter what, I couldn't wind up on a basketball court.

I walked around for maybe fifteen minutes, until I couldn't take it anymore. I turned around all at once, and headed for the Circle. I was cursing myself all the way there for being so stupid. But if I couldn't play, I at least had to see what was going on without me.

I jumped the little fence that separates the sidewalk from the grass, so nobody would see me coming. Then

I poked my head around the corner of one of the buildings. Probably every guy who ever had a beef in that park checked the place out the same way. The Circle was mobbed. Somebody had just made a shot to win the game. Half of the players were walking off of the court, and a new crew was coming on. I looked over every part of the park twice; Marcus wasn't there.

When I got back home, my mom had a sour look on her face and said there was a message on the answering machine for me. We had stopped picking up the phone, in case it was a reporter or St. John's. Until everything calmed down, my dad wanted Mr. Golub to do all the talking. And so did I.

Before I hit the playback button, my mother rushed upstairs. She didn't want any part of hearing what was on that tape again.

"Eddie, it's Rebecca. My parents saw the article in the paper and freaked out. They won't let me go out with you tonight. Don't call back here or anything. I'll call you tomorrow afternoon when I can get out of the house. We can do something then. I promise. Bye."

I explained everything to Rebecca after the story came out. That it was all a mistake. How after the cops decided it was Marcus, they went looking for somebody close to him. She was worried for me, and I was relieved that she didn't treat me like a criminal. But I didn't really know her parents, and wasn't surprised by their reaction.

The next morning, the phone rang just after eleven o'clock. My mom and Rose were at church, and my dad was working overtime. I didn't want Rebecca to get the answering machine again, so I picked the phone up on the second ring.

"Eddie Russo, this is Steve Jenkins, the coach of the basketball program at St. John's," the deep voice said.

"Good morning, Coach Jenkins," I answered slowly.

He said that hearing back from my lawyer was fine, but that he really wanted to talk to me or my parents. He asked me how I was holding up under the pressure, and if I was still going to school every day. I told him that I was on track to graduate. And nothing would stop me.

"Once you sign that letter, and commit to St. John's, you're a member of our family. If you ever need somebody to talk to, you can come to me or one of the school guidance counselors. We're always going to be here for you," he said. "But remember, a felony conviction is serious business, and would cost you this scholarship."

I told him how much I appreciated everything, and that my lawyer had it all under control. And I'd be ready to start in the fall.

When we were finished, I felt like I had just walked through a minefield without taking a single bad step. I was so pumped up that I ran around the house practicing layups and jumping off the balls of my feet. But when I finally started to come back down, I felt sick. And I hated every lie that had come out of my mouth.

On Monday, I was all geared up for practice. The starters scrimmaged against the scrubs. And I made sure our side was going all out. I hit my first six shots and was really feeling it. My next jumper fell short off the front lip of the rim. So I charged the basket and grabbed my own rebound. I jammed the ball home over Preston, and shot him a look like he didn't even belong on the court with me.

The ball kicked loose between a dozen legs. There were a bunch of arms just reaching for it. I hit the floor and hauled it in. It cost me some skin off my right knee and elbow. But it was worth it. I was setting the tone and everyone on my squad was following me. It was flowing good between me and Marcus, too. The starters never let up, and we just crushed them.

Casey watched without saying a word. When he finally blew the whistle for us to stop, he said, "That's the way to get it done, boys!"

I tried to give Marcus a pep talk on the way home. I started out with the playoffs and worked my way over to how the case would blow up in the DA's face. But the second I quit talking, Marcus cleared his throat.

"Eddie, I don't think taking the case to trial is going to work for me," he blurted out. "Parker knows it was me. And I don't think I can pretend it wasn't. I don't want to screw this up for you. Maybe your lawyer is just smarter than mine. Ms. Torres doesn't think there's a thing she can say to make me look good. I need to take whatever she can get me."

I drop-kicked my book bag halfway down the block. I felt like Marcus was just giving up. Then something snapped, and I just went off on him.

"Whatever she can get for you! What about me, my brother? You want to plead guilty. But that's only going to hurt my case. Do you get some kind of points from the DA for that?" I yelled at him.

Before the last word had left my mouth, Marcus exploded.

"You lousy little shit!" he screamed, wrapping both of his hands around my jacket collar. He drove me back against the side of a brick building. And I felt the air pop out of my lungs when I hit.

"We got into this mess together. But it's just me paying for it. And I haven't complained one fucking inch about it," he seethed, with his face pressed up against mine. "And all you want to know from me is how clean *I* can keep *you*."

I didn't move a muscle, or say anything. I just tried to look into his eyes. But he was so close that I could barely make them out. Then Marcus loosened his grip, and stepped back.

I felt lower than the curb—and stupid, too. I looked around to see if anybody on the street was listening. There were a couple of people who turned their heads, but they all just kept walking. I caught my breath, and took a step closer to Marcus.

"I know I've been seeing it all my way," I told him. "It's just been hard, all right?"

We didn't talk for the rest of the way home. But I listened to the sound of his footsteps. They never slowed down or picked up once. He just kept the same steady pace. Right before we split up, I gave Marcus a pound and said, "Black and White through thick and thin."

He nodded his head as he pulled his fist back from mine. "That hasn't changed from my side one time," he said. "Not one time."

That night, Mr. Golub called. I heard the sound of his voice on the answering machine before my dad picked up. It was dry, without any emotion. So I knew that I had been indicted by the grand jury. Dad held the phone to his ear and listened to him talk. Every couple of seconds, he gave Golub an "all right" or "okay." When they were through, my dad broke the news.

It was like when my grandpa had been sick for a long time, and everybody knew that he was going to die. Nobody was shocked. We were all pretty much prepared for it. It was the same with getting indicted. I was surprised how well my mom took it. She shook her head and her eyes got wet. But she didn't fall apart. I tried not to react to it, because it didn't matter much. I was going to face a lot worse before it was finished. I just wished Marcus would fight it like I was.

Casey spent half of our next practice at the blackboard, diagraming all the plays he wanted to run that Friday. It felt more like school than basketball. Everybody had to take notes on where to go for every play. We already had it all in our notebooks at home. But Casey wanted us to write it all out again.

"From your fingers to your brains," Casey said. "We'll do it on paper, then walk it through on the court."

We hardly broke a sweat. But it was one of the toughest practices we had all year. We walked around each other in circles, one step at a time. Me and Marcus did a slow dance together through every offensive set. We even had to pass an invisible ball back and forth.

And after a while, my arms started to get heavy.

On the way home, Marcus froze in his tracks. He stood in front of me, face-to-face, and told me that he was still going to take a plea.

"You're just playing the cops' game," I said.

"It's not a game for me anymore," said Marcus.

"No, because you're giving up. You're quitting on me, and it's making me look worse," I told him.

"Listen, it was *your* gun, and *your* mistake," he came back.

"And I asked *you* to hold it that night, but *you* quit on me then, too," I said, turning away from him.

It all stopped as fast as it came, and we just walked. But I knew from the sound of his voice that nothing I could say would make a difference.

After Marcus left, I wondered how it would feel to be free of this whole thing, or at least tell everyone the truth. I stood on the corner of my block and looked out into the traffic. Then I pulled up everything I'd been thinking about and feeling. I opened my mouth wide to scream. But not a sound came out.

I was watching TV in the living room when Rose came downstairs. She made me turn it off and started an introduction using her hand as a microphone.

"Ladies and gentlemen, Long Island City High School

presents Senior Night," she said out loud. "We'd like to acknowledge the parents of our senior athletes for all the contributions they've made."

My mom and dad started down the stairs, arm in arm. Mom was wearing a maroon dress with a blue-and-white bow. Dad had on his black suit that he only wore to funerals and weddings. When they reached the bottom, Rose pretended to snap pictures.

Senior Night was usually the last home game of the year. But once we clinched home court advantage for the playoffs, the seniors on the team voted to have it before our first playoff game. Then the gym would really be rocking that night.

The lights in the gym get completely turned out, and everything is pitch black. A white spotlight comes on, and each senior player walks his parents out to center court. Then the player gives his mother a bouquet of roses, and everyone applauds. My mom had been looking forward to Senior Night since I was a freshman. It was a way to say thank you to her in front of everybody.

My dad fidgeted with his suit. He kept running his finger between his neck and his shirt collar, trying to breathe. "How am I supposed to sit at a basketball game in a monkey suit?" he said, before he pulled off his tie to watch TV.

Marcus showed up at school the next day wearing his suit. I saw him walk into English class and did a double-take. He said that he was going down to the DA's office with his mother later on. His lawyer was going to be there, too, to read over the plea before he signed it.

He took a deal to be home in nineteen months. He said it could even get shortened if he didn't get into anything stupid while he was locked up. The state was giving him three weeks to report to jail. Marcus laughed and said that was just enough extra time for us to win the city championship. Casey knew all about it, and cleared Marcus to miss practice that day. That way he could still start in the playoff game on Friday.

All through class, I watched Marcus out of the corner of my eye. My stomach was twisting into knots.

Kids were still reading their essays in class. Ms. Sussman hadn't called on either me or Marcus yet. There weren't that many kids left to go. I knew that I'd be on the spot soon.

There were just five minutes left in the period when she called my name. I started to read as fast as I could. I didn't want to hear myself with Marcus sitting there that way. But Ms. Sussman stopped me in the middle of the first sentence. She told me to stand up while I was reading, and to slow down. So I had to go back to the beginning.

"I'd like people to remember me as somebody they could depend on. No matter what happens, I'm always right there. I'm not the kind of person who walks away when things get tough. I don't care if it's crunch time on the basketball court or the last play of a football game, I'm willing to put myself on the line. . . ."

BLACK

Connelly pulled me out of science class. He just walked in while some kid was giving an answer and yelled out my name.

"Let's go!" he snorted to me.

Connelly kept two steps behind me. I peeked back and thought his knees were going to buckle from all the weight. I heard his breathing and heavy footsteps follow me down a flight of stairs to the front desk.

Jefferson was there talking with my mother.

"You have to sign him out," Connelly said to her as he wiped the sweat from his forehead.

Jefferson walked us outside and told my mother, "I know he's made some mistakes. But that's what adolescents do. Marcus is the type of young man who's going to learn from what he did wrong. He's going to pick himself back up and succeed. And one day, other kids from this neighborhood are going to look up to him for that."

My mother let out a long breath and said, "It's going to be a test for him, every day from now on."

Then Jefferson turned to me and said, "You don't know how lucky you are to have this strong woman in your corner."

I told him that I already did.

"No, you only think that you know," Jefferson came back. "You haven't seen enough at your age to really understand what it means. When you become a father one day, you'll see better. You'll understand everything your mother's done for you."

Ms. Torres met us at the DA's office on Union Turnpike, a few blocks from the Queens courthouse. She looked over the plea and gave me the okay to sign it. I pushed the paper down hard against the desk. I started out using big letters. But by the time I got to the end of my name, the letters were less than half that size. I picked the pen up off the paper and everything inside of me felt more settled. It was finally over.

I had three weeks before getting shipped upstate. After that, I wouldn't see my mother or sister for close to two years, except through a piece of glass in a prison visiting room. I wouldn't be running with Eddie, either. I'd be standing on my own. I'd be doing my time with adults, who could be locked up for anything. And I knew I'd probably have to fight to show them I wasn't anybody's herb. Deep down, that had me shook.

The school guidance counselor gave me a note to bring to all my teachers. They could write down what I did for them in the first half of this semester. Then when I got into a jail school upstate, I could finish classes. I could get my diploma, or take the GED exam.

The next day, I saw Eddie before English class. He was waiting for me to say how it all went with the DA. I could see how anxious he was about it. But I wasn't in the mood to replay the whole scene for him.

"So?" Eddie asked.

"It's over for me." I kept it short.

Two girls from class came up to us, and asked me how long it was going to be before I had to go to jail. Eddie looked at me like I'd been talking it up all over school. But the girls said there was a piece in the newspaper about me pleading guilty.

Casey met the team at the locker room door before practice. He pulled me off to the side and told me to chill in his office. He told everyone else to dress warm and run laps around the school for the next twenty minutes. Casey said he didn't know what was going on, but the principal wanted to see us both.

Ms. Randolph was on the phone with some kid's parent, and pointed to the two chairs in front of her desk. She said the kid's name right in front of me, and what he did in class to get suspended. I remembered the kid from the tenth grade, but I didn't want to hear a damn thing about anybody else's troubles.

The second she put down the phone, Ms. Randolph started talking to Casey and me. She said her part like she was reading it off the wall behind us, and the words weren't really hers.

"The Queens Superintendent of High Schools saw the story on you in the newspaper today. He called to remind me that with your conviction you are to be removed from any extracurricular activities while you're still here," she said, raising her cheeks to add some sympathy to it. "Not that I necessarily agree with it, but I must remove you from the basketball team."

When she was finished, she pushed her chair back, like I might attack her. But I had a good hold on myself. Anyway, I wanted to cry more than I wanted to pound somebody.

"What? What did you say?" Casey called out in shock. "He's free to walk around the streets until he starts serving his time. But he can't play high school basketball? That's insane!"

"You have to understand. Marcus has pled guilty to a violent crime. What if there's a scuffle on the court, and even in self-defense, he injures someone," she said with a straight face. "There could be a lawsuit against the Board of Education. Mr. Casey, you more than anyone should be sensitive to what can go tragically wrong in these situations."

Casey flew up from his chair and said, "Are you comparing Marcus to that animal who killed Jason Taylor? Is that what you're doing? You weren't even at this school back then."

"I am not comparing Marcus to anyone," Ms. Randolph shot back. "Don't put words in my mouth, Mr. Casey!"

I had a sick feeling in the pit of my stomach that kept on getting worse. Maybe I didn't stab somebody to death because he was a different color than me. But I helped rob people at gunpoint, and almost got someone's head blown off. And now I was going to prison, just like that bastard who killed Jason.

When we got back upstairs, Casey held a team meeting. He was still steaming and his face had turned completely red. The sweat was pouring off kids from running laps. Eddie was looking at me in my street clothes and shaking his head. He probably had it figured out before anybody else. Casey turned to me and pushed his lips together. Before he could start, I told them all that I was off the team.

"Because I pleaded guilty, they won't let me play," I said. "I screwed up this season for everybody. I probably could have waited another two or three weeks before I took the plea. I'm sorry. I just didn't know about the rule."

"You don't have to be sorry to us, my brother," said X, shifting his eyes over to Eddie. "You got caught out there and now you're paying the price. At least you're man enough to stand up for it. Some guys will never have that in them."

Most of the team started clapping after X had his say. But Eddie just stood there with both hands in his pockets.

The principal said I couldn't stay to watch practice or sit on the bench for the playoff game the next night. My teammates said they would clap loudest for me when I walked out with my mother for Senior Night. And they'd tell kids around school to do the same.

I thought the only time I wouldn't be with the LIC team was when I graduated and had a place to play in college. But I left Eddie and everyone else in the gym, and went down the back stairs alone. My mother was pissed as anything over it. She said they were treating me like a convict already.

But that night she ironed her best dress, and Sabrina's, too.

"People at Senior Night are going to know that your family is still proud of you. The principal can't make all your hard work for that team just disappear," my mother said, snapping her fingers.

The news about me being off the team traveled slow. The whole next day at school, kids kept coming up and wishing me good luck in the game. It was like getting kicked in the ass, over and over.

Rose found me in the library. She wanted to tell me what kind of raw deal she thought I got from the principal. I told her it didn't really matter anyway. My life had already changed, and I was going to have to deal with whatever people put in my way from now on.

She apologized for the way her parents were talking about me at home. And for them thinking that I put all of this onto Eddie. She hugged me tight, and everything hard inside me melted down a little.

Eddie didn't say much to me in English class, except that he couldn't believe the Board of Education pulled the plug on "Black and White." Ms.

Sussman still had kids reading their essays, and I was one of the last to go. I stood up and read out loud. I wasn't concentrating on anything but the words on the paper in front of me. I was sailing straight through it, without even listening to the sound of my voice. Then right before the ending, I missed a word and had to stop for a second. It was like waking up out of a daydream, and everybody's looking at you.

"In the end, I'd like people to say that I tried to be honest with them. I want them to remember the real Marcus Brown. Not the ballplayer or anybody else. That way they'll have a clear picture in their head about me, and not have to guess," I finished and sat back down.

In math class, the teacher had us working in groups of four. Eddie had his desk turned around to face me. We mostly talked about the game, and let the other two kids with us do all the problems.

"It's all on you tonight," I told Eddie.

Usually two hundred people showed up for a Friday night game. But for the playoffs and Senior Night, Eddie thought we'd get at least four hundred people in the stands. We were playing Aviation High School. They were the last squad to make the playoffs. During the first week of the season, we beat them by almost thirty points. But they'd got a lot better since then, and won just enough games to get in.

Eddie and me talked about our families being next to each other before they walked onto the court that night. We both knew that it was going to be tense.

"I'd rather face the DA and judge together than your mother," Eddie said.

Eddie met up with Rebecca after class. I was heading out the front door alone when Jefferson called me over to his desk. He reached into his pocket and took out twelve dollars.

"It's a six-dollar ride from the Ravenswood Houses to here. I want you to take your mother back and forth by cab tonight," he said, handing me the money.

I didn't want Jefferson's money. But I could tell right off that he wasn't going to take it back. So I closed a tight fist around the bills. I started to tell him how grateful I was. But Jefferson stopped me in the middle and said, "Every young brother needs a little help along the way. I'm just paying back what came down to me."

Sabrina was really excited about Senior Night. My mother made her a fancy red dress with lace skirts, one on top of the other. It was finished more than a month ago, and Sabrina had been trying it on every Friday night since. With her hair piled up high, she looked just like a princess in it. My mother had on a long black dress with heels. Around her neck, she wore a string of white pearls that my grandmother gave her before she passed away.

Both of them were watching the clock, and telling me that we were going to be late. I kept pushing them off. I ran for the phone the second it rang. A man on the other end said our cab was waiting outside. My mother smiled when I told her.

The driver must have been wondering why my mother and sister were dressed so nice, and I was wearing maroon sweats. Sabrina talked about being scared to walk out in front of the crowd the whole ride over. And by the time we got to LIC, the driver was going on to my sister about not being nervous. He even wished the team good luck.

There was still an hour before the game, and the players were just starting to warm up. The end of the first row was saved for the senior parents. I never left my mother and sister to walk over to Casey or the team. But once they started to run a layup line right in front of where we were sitting, everyone was coming up to us.

On Eddie's first run through the line, he took a few steps over. I got up to meet him halfway. He gave me a pound and nodded his head in my mother's direction. She pulled Sabrina in tight to say something, and Eddie moved forward on the line. I don't think either one of them looked the other in the face for more than a second. Every time Eddie came through after that, he was focused on the basket, with his game face on.

The stands filled up fast. Other parents moved into the seats next to us. Casey's wife was hugging everybody. Then Rose showed up with Eddie's mother and father, and took the last seats in the row. Rose and me kept looking at each other over everyone's heads. I wished that she was sitting right next to me. But there was no way.

Jefferson and Connelly were there, too. They were busy checking kids' IDs and making sure the crowd stayed cool. I made sure to catch Jefferson's eye, just to show him that I was glued to my family.

We were wearing our home whites. Aviation was dressed in green and gold. I could see myself out on the court, moving through the layup line. And every time somebody passed Eddie the ball, my hands started to twitch a little. The only times I ever watched the team play, I was sitting on the bench, waiting to get back into the game. I didn't know how I was going to handle sitting in the stands. The game hadn't even started, and I wanted to jump up out of my seat and take off running down the court.

After a while, the president of the senior council arranged us in order along the sideline. The ceremony was almost ready to start. Eddie and the other seniors came over to walk their parents across the court. The lights got turned way down, until it was almost black inside the gym. Music piped in over the PA system, and kids in the stands started to hoot and holler. Ms. Randolph stepped into the white spotlight and welcomed everybody to Senior Night. Then she handed the microphone over to Casey, who gave a speech from the heart.

"Our student-athletes invest a lot of time and effort in representing Long Island City High School," Casey said. "That added burden is also felt at home, where the parents of our student-athletes must work even harder to give their children support. Tonight we honor those parents."

The first family made their way out to center court. The senior council president handed our player a bouquet of roses. He gave them to his mother and kissed her with everybody cheering. The next family was already moving when Ms. Randolph planted herself in front of me.

"I told you that you couldn't be a part of any

extracurricular activities. That included Senior Night, Mr. Brown," she said. "Your family can go out there. But not you!"

"My son is walking with me!" my mother told her, flat out.

Ms. Randolph started to argue. But my mother's words turned me rock solid. I could have walked through a hundred Ms. Randolphs with her words running through my head.

Jefferson and Connelly were in the middle of it now. I looked back over my shoulder and could see Eddie handing his mother her bouquet. My mother started to move forward with me holding one hand and Sabrina the other. But Ms. Randolph blocked our way. I wanted to boot her across the court for disrespecting my mother like that. Jefferson tried his best to get Ms. Randolph to step aside.

That's when some black kids in the bleachers screamed she was a racist. Connelly stormed over and told them all to shut up. A girl oinked right in his face and called him a fat pig. Connelly lost it and jerked her hard by the collar. Some dude slugged Connelly in the mouth, and a bunch of kids piled on top of him. Jefferson rushed over to save his partner's ass, and everything in that corner of the stands just broke loose.

When the lights didn't come on, kids started throwing things in the dark. Casey's voice boomed over the PA for everybody to stay calm. Something hard whistled right past my ear. I turned my back to the crowd and shielded my mother and sister inside my arms. Sabrina dug her nails into my stomach.

"Don't let them hurt me!" she cried.

Eddie and his parents were standing in the spotlight out at center court. I knew that Rose was taking pictures from the first row. But I didn't see her anywhere.

The lights finally got turned up, but that didn't stop anything. Connelly had wrestled some kid out of the pack, and was beating the shit out of him. Jefferson had to hook Connelly around the throat and slam him to the floor to get him to stop.

Lots of people ran out onto the court, just to get clear of that mess. Eddie and his parents got swallowed up by that crowd. I lost sight of them. I saw Rose run past with tears coming down her face. If my arms were long enough, I would have reached out and held on to her, too.

Casey stayed on the microphone. He kept begging people to do the right thing, and most of them did. Then the cops showed up and cleared out the whole gym. They even had to separate Jefferson and

Connelly, who were pushing and shoving at each other now. There was blood running from Connelly's nose down to his chin. Jefferson's uniform shirt was ripped across the middle. Ms. Randolph was walking in a daze from one end of the gym to the other. And my mother was giving her lip every step of the way.

On the way out, I saw the broken glass on the gym floor. The case that held Jason's jersey got busted open. His uniform top was hanging loose, pinned up by only one shoulder. I reached my hand in through the sharp edges, and hooked it back on right.

The cops wouldn't let anyone stand out in front of the school, either. There was an ambulance parked outside and a bunch of black-and-whites with all their lights flashing. So we started walking home as soon as we hit the street. Sabrina looked like she just woke up from a nightmare. She was walking with the side of her face pressed up under my mother's arm.

My mother's steps were slow and even. Then she started to shake her head as we walked. She turned to me and said, "For better or worse, child, you'll find out everything you want to know about this world."

WHITE

Mom didn't stop crying until she found Rose. We were all standing in the middle of the court, looking at each other. I had seen my mom and dad every day for as far back as I could remember. Somewhere in my head, I had an outline of their faces. Maybe I'd been using that for too long, instead of really seeing them. They looked older and more scared now than I'd ever seen them before.

The cops only let the players, coaches, and refs stay in the gym, and moved everybody else outside. I lost sight of Marcus and couldn't spot him anywhere. My mother was holding on to her bouquet so tight that some of the roses got crushed. There were loose petals stuck to her dress and on the floor around her feet. I walked with my family over to the doors, and a woman cop pushed them through.

Casey was down on one knee, sweeping up glass off the gym floor. The principal was hanging over him. You could tell that they were arguing, but their voices never got loud enough for anyone else to hear. When he finished with the glass, Casey stood up and walked right past her to a big aluminum trash can.

If it wasn't for Ms. Randolph, me and Marcus would be playing side by side right now. My parents and everybody else would be in the stands cheering. And Marcus's mother would have walked across the floor to get her bouquet. I wanted to tell her off in front of everyone. But the truth was that I was more to blame than anyone.

The refs gave us ten minutes to get loose again. Aviation was running a layup line with their coach out on the court watching them. Casey was still busy making sure everything was back together. Our guys were all taking jumpers, and we had a half dozen balls going up at the same time.

I was standing in the corner pounding the ball against the floor. First with my right hand, and then with the left. I guess I just wanted to feel like everything was still the same—that I could dribble without looking down at the ball, and that it would always come back up into my hand.

"Hey, White, you gonna play a big game for your boy out in the street tonight, or are you gonna turn your back on us, too?" X asked me with a real smirk.

"Just watch me," I answered him.

A security officer brought Rebecca and the rest of the cheerleaders back up to the gym. But the other coach said it wasn't fair that his pep squad couldn't get inside, and Casey agreed. The girls shook their pom-poms on the way out, and Rebecca blew me a kiss.

Right before we went out on the court, Casey pulled us together and said, "This is the part where we just play ball and all that other garbage can't touch us."

"No disrespect, Coach," X came back. "But how come it's always the black man that has to forget about all the bullshit."

Moses told X to let it go, and Casey stayed quiet for a few seconds until it passed. After Casey finished up, we put our hands together and shouted, "T-E-A-M!" But the sound of our voices barely carried out of the huddle.

The ref tossed the ball up at center court, and Big Andre won the tap. Preston ran down the loose ball and put it into my hands. I found X open down low. He took a tough fade-away jumper. But he hit it. The next time we had the ball, X forced up a shot with a defender all over him. He hit that one, too. I watched X run back on defense. It looked like every emotion in the world was racing through him at the same time. And he didn't have to hide or be ashamed of any one of them.

I needed to get into the flow. So I took the first

open shot I could find. The ball went halfway down into the rim, and then rattled back out. Before I could get my hands on the ball again, X took two more shots and missed them both by a mile. Then he got frustrated and smacked an Aviation kid—who had a clear path to the basket—hard across the arms. The refs whistled X for an intentional foul, and Casey got on him from the side-line about it. But X put both of his hands out in front of him to say that he had himself under control.

Half of the first quarter was gone and I didn't have a single point yet. We were down by a basket when I stole a pass. Preston was running alone ahead of me. I never once thought about giving up the ball. I ran right by him to the hoop and got my first two points.

Every play we ran was out of sync. Without the ball in Marcus's hands, we were a step behind on every-thing.

The kid Andre was guarding knocked Moses flat with a blind screen. Moses screamed at Andre all the way back up court for not letting him know it was com-ing. Then X missed another shot he should have never taken. The first quarter ended with the score tied 14–14.

When we got back to the bench, Casey didn't say a thing about strategy. Instead, he said we should clear our minds and try to focus more. He told X not to put so much pressure on himself. Then Casey pulled me off to the side.

"Eddie, this is your team now," he said, with a tight grip on my shoulder. "It's up to you to keep them all together."

I stepped back onto the court, and all of a sudden, I started to cry. For a second, I just lost control. Marcus, the cops, the bus driver, my grandpa—they were all fighting to get out. I shut my eyes. They were stinging from the salt. And I hoped it looked like I was wiping away sweat, instead of tears. Then I raised my arms and felt the air flowing through my chest. I looked up at the scoreboard, and just shook it all off.

I made a basket to start the second quarter, and then I caught fire. I hit five straight shots. But Aviation was making shots, too, and we were winning by only four points. Then the other coach brought a player with fresh legs off the bench to run with me. He was some kind of track star with long arms. His face looked a little like Marcus's. And that got into my head. He tried to stay within two feet of me, with his face up in mine. He was going all out every second to keep close. I could feel his breath on my skin.

It was almost impossible to get the ball with that kid

guarding me. It would have been different with Marcus on the court. And Preston wasn't a slick enough passer to find me when I did get free. I didn't get another shot off for the rest of the half. We went back to the locker room with only a two-point lead—36–34.

Casey was as calm as could be, and went over what the other team was trying to do to us. But it was our own mistakes that kept the game close, and everybody knew it.

"You got to put a lock on that trigger finger, X," Andre said. "You can't take all those tough shots."

"White was on a roll out there, just get him the ball," said Moses.

"These guys can't beat us," I said, heading for bathroom. "We're just better than them."

I ran the cold water in the white sink, and splashed it onto my wrists and neck to keep cool. That's when X followed me inside. I could see his face behind mine in the mirror. "You just find a way to ditch your black shadow out there, before he follows you home and climbs into bed with you," X told me.

We got back onto the court to warm up, and the refs were covering Jason's case with a blanket. They didn't want anybody to get cut on the broken glass hanging off of it. When they were finished, Casey put two fingers to his lips and touched the outside of the blanket before he came back to the bench.

"Play like you know you can," Casey told us. "That's all anyone can ask of you."

The track star got a good rest during halftime, and was ready to go all over again. He wasn't even part of their offense. When they had the ball, he just stayed close to me. That way I couldn't get a head start on him going back the other way.

No matter what we did, we couldn't pull away from them. We would go up by three or four points. Then they'd come right back and take the lead on us. All I had to do to swing the whole game around was get my hands on the ball. But I couldn't.

I kept running harder and harder. My black shadow started to lose a step. I even got away from him one play and made a basket. That's when the Aviation coach pulled him out of the game, and sent in another kid to take his place. This one didn't look anything at all like Marcus, except that he was black, too. He wasn't as fast as the first kid. But he was fresh, and followed me everywhere. Three minutes later, when that kid started to slow down, their coach brought another player off the bench to run with me.

We went into the fourth quarter down by four points. If the stands had been filled with people, no one would have believed their eyes, not even Aviation's fans. My black shadow came back into the game, and locked me right up again. I didn't touch the ball on offense for the next four or five minutes. Nothing went right for us. We were losing by six points late in the game. I got the ball in the corner, and my black shadow stripped it from me. Before he could take off the other way with it, I tackled him around the waist with both arms.

The two refs, in their black-and-white-striped shirts, pointed at me and blew their whistles. I raised my hand high to the scorer's table, and one of refs called out my number for the foul.

I couldn't watch the clock ticking down. But when the kids on the Aviation sideline started hugging, I knew the time was running out. I didn't care about the score anymore. I just wanted to get off one last shot. My black shadow didn't let me near the ball until the buzzer sounded. We lost 60 to 49. And I walked off the court with the ball in my hands.

Back in the locker room, Casey told us to put the game aside for a while and try to enjoy the weekend. He said that he'd save all the speeches for Monday. Nobody argued with him. Kids were just sitting in front of their lockers, stunned that we got knocked out of the playoffs so early.

I was pissed as hell. I didn't want to be anywhere around those guys. I couldn't believe that a kid with nothing going for him but two good legs could stop me. I got dressed and headed down the back stairs. I almost expected to see Marcus waiting outside. But he wasn't there. My dad was waiting for me. Rebecca and the other cheerleaders were there, too. The Aviation squad had come down celebrating. So they already knew.

BLACK

I woke up early the next morning and the sun was out full. Sabrina was too scared to sleep alone. She spent the night with my mother in her bed. The two of them were still asleep under the covers. I got dressed and grabbed a ball without making a peep. Then I headed down to the Circle.

It wasn't even eight o'clock yet. The first handful of players usually don't show up until after nine. But I was glad to be out there by myself. I found a flat piece of ground where I could put the ball down and it wouldn't roll off. Then I went out to the center of the court and started to stretch. I closed my eyes, leaning all the way back. For a second, everything was black. Then the orange light came pouring underneath my eyelids. I could feel the warm sun on my face.

I was a million miles away from the gym the night before. My mind was clear and focused on everything in front of me. I flipped the ball through the rim with my right hand, and caught it in my left.

I kept going back and forth between hands, putting up little shots. I had a good rhythm going. And as soon as the ball hit my hand, it was back up in the air again. I started to move around the court, making shots. I'd take off with a burst of speed, then throw on the brakes. I was going fast and slow at the same time, moving inside and out. I worked up a real sweat that rolled down my face and dripped to the ground.

I didn't expect to see Eddie. There was just too much going on for him to play out here. Other guys started showing up one by one. When we got enough bodies, they chose up sides. I heard my name get called first. After that, it didn't matter to me. I figured out the sides on our first trip up court. I saw who was turned towards me, and who was facing the other way.

It was an okay game. A lot of players who are just so-so show up early to get their licks in before the Circle gets too tough. But I wasn't holding back an inch. I was blowing by kids like they were standing still. Nobody on the other team wanted to guard me. My squad won the first three games, and I didn't slow down a beat. The next team was coming onto the court when I saw Moses and X walk into the park. I was waiting for them to say something about the night before. But they both sat at the end of the bench, looking at me like they'd let me down for everything.

I thought that maybe something else had jumped off after I left. That maybe something bad happened to Eddie or Casey. It went right by me the first time Moses said the team got beat. I had to reach back and put the words to the look on their faces.

I couldn't believe it. But it didn't seem important enough anymore to stress about, either. Win or lose, nothing was any different for me. Only the playoffs were over.

I walked onto the court and made the first three baskets of the new game.

My squad had point-game at 14–6. That's when I saw Rose at the edge of the park. She was standing between buildings, watching me play. I told X to take my spot, and walked off. The kids on my team made a fuss about me leaving and were calling after me. Rose put a hand out in front of her for me to stay. But I didn't pay attention to any of it. I grabbed Rose's hand and we walked out of the Circle together.

Rose asked about my mother and sister. I told her they got through the night in one piece. After we got past what Ms. Randolph did, and that the team lost, we didn't mention either one of those things again.

"I just wanted to come out and see you play," she said.

We went around the block one time, then turned up towards Steinway Street. I held on to Rose's hand all the way, until she pointed to show me something in a store window. After that, I just settled for walking with her shoulder next to mine.

Rose said she didn't think her parents would let her take the bus upstate to visit me. I told her I'd have to write her letters instead. She smiled at that, and said she'd answer them all. Then Rose asked me if I thought Eddie would go to jail, too.

"He's innocent until somebody proves different in court," I said. "That can be hard to do sometimes."

On the way back, Rose turned inside a flower shop, and I followed in behind her. She smelled lots of different flowers. And I put my nose to every one she did. Rose bought a dozen red roses. The salesman wrapped the stems in silver paper. Rose handed them to me with the water still dripping out from the bottom. I carried them all the way home for her.

On the corner of Rose's block, I tried to hand her back the bouquet. But she just laughed at me and said, "They're for your mother, Marcus. To make up for the ones she didn't get last night."

Rose kissed me good-bye and started for her house. Then she turned back around and caught me watching her from behind. And the sunlight shined in her eyes when she smiled at me.

My mother loved the roses. But I wouldn't take credit for them, and told her that they were from Rose.

Most of that night, I thought about Rose. I thought about what it would be like to hold her tight and kiss her for real. I dreamed she was lying in my arms, soft and warm.

My mother said that I should go to church with her and Sabrina. I really didn't want to, but I didn't want to let her down anymore, either. I hadn't been to church since the Christmas I started high school. That's when my mother told me I was old enough to make up my own mind about going, and old enough to stay home alone on a Sunday morning.

Reverend Hawkins was the only preacher I ever knew. He had been there since I was born, and even baptized me. He remembered my father growing up, too. Sometimes he'd tell stories about the kids who hung out on the church corner in the old days. My father was one of them.

I got two phone calls from my father since he'd

left. Both of them were on my birthday. The first time, my mother just handed me the phone. She whispered who it was to me, so my sister wouldn't hear. My father had the deepest voice I ever heard. I told him about playing ball and junior high. Before I knew it, he was saying good-bye.

Two years ago, he called again. Only I picked up the phone myself. He said, "Marcus, this is your father." He told me he could tell how I was growing by the sound of my voice. I talked about getting a scholarship and turning pro one day. He said he wasn't surprised I was going to be somebody. He never said out loud he loved me, so I didn't go there, either. But the call still felt good, like he was right there with me.

Reverend Hawkins had passed away since the last time I went to church. The new reverend was from Guyana. His accent was thick, and I couldn't understand half of what he said during the service. Maybe a lot of people couldn't, or it just took more practice hearing him. I mostly paid attention to the light coming through the stained glass windows. The same sky could be red, yellow, or green depending on where you looked. I hardly ever prayed. But I asked God to look after my mother and sister while I was away upstate. Then I put in a word for Jefferson, and everything he did for me.

After the service, my mother needed to go food shopping. So we walked down to the C-Town supermarket. Sabrina still got a kick out of seeing the big plaster animals on the roof. They had a white chicken with red feathers, and a black-and-brown cow staring down at you. There used to be a giant pig, too. But it got blown off the roof in a storm, and the store never fixed it.

Sabrina ran to get her own cart to push. She was making car noises with it, and racing up and down the aisles. I was going slow, pushing the cart while my mother dropped groceries into it. Then I challenged Sabrina to a race. She was ahead of me, but I was going to let her win from the start. She turned the corner too fast and almost ran into some old man. I was far back enough to look like I had nothing to do with it. But my mother threw a fit at the both of us anyway, and made Sabrina get rid of her cart.

We turned down the last aisle, and came out by the checkout lines. I was the first one to see it coming. They were heading towards us at the same speed we were moving to them.

"Sweet Jesus, I don't want this today!" my mother cried up to the ceiling.

Eddie's mother was pushing the shopping cart. Eddie and his father were walking a step or two behind her. Everyone just froze where they were for a second. It was like the negative to some picture that somebody put away and forgot about, with us in black and them in white.

We were maybe ten feet apart from each other. I looked Eddie in the face, and then my mother. Before anybody could move, my mother asked Eddie, "Isn't that my son's jacket you borrowed? From when yours got stolen that night?"

Eddie looked down at the jacket over his chest and arms. His father moved over to stand in front of his mother.

"Make sure to return it real soon," my mother said. "Marcus won't be with us too much longer. He's going to prison, you know."

Eddie put his hand up around the zipper. But my mother grabbed Sabrina by the arm and rolled her cart away. Eddie brought his eyes up and stared at me, like he didn't know what he could do. I wanted to say something, and even started to move my lips. But I couldn't find any words that made sense.

I put my hands in my pockets and followed after my mother.

The rest of the day, I could see that speech she gave Eddie flying around in my mother's head. She was doing housework with a real attitude. The words were going back and forth inside of her. Sometimes her lips would move without making a sound. Only this time, that speech was longer, and maybe somebody had something to say back to her. A couple of times, one or two of the words popped out of her mouth. But she'd jerk her body in a different direction to close the lid tight again.

I saw the scrub brush sitting in the bathroom, and thought about my one day cleaning toilets on Rikers Island. I could hear my mother working hard in the kitchen, and felt ashamed. I didn't want the next toilet I cleaned to belong to the state. So I picked up the brush and started at ours.

Both Jefferson and Connelly were missing from the front desk at school on Monday. I asked one of the other school safety officers what happened. He said the both of them were transferred to different office buildings run by the Board of Education, until all the charges got sorted out. Some kid at the game was charging Connelly with assault. Connelly was pressing charges against Jefferson for hitting him. For now, neither one of them was allowed to be around kids in a school.

I felt bad for Jefferson getting a rap like that, and

having to prove he didn't do anything wrong. Maybe he took an extra-hard swipe at Connelly. But that bastard deserved it. I wanted to go down to where Jefferson was and tell somebody in charge all the good things he ever did for kids. Then I'd probably have to say I was going to jail for pulling a stickup, and nobody would believe me anymore.

WHITE

All the way home from the supermarket, my mom was crying. She tried hard to hold it in, and lowered her head so we couldn't see how red her eyes were. My dad kept trying to make small talk with her, pretending that everything was okay. But every time mom tried to answer him, she broke out in a sob instead. I wanted to tell her that everything was all right. But it wasn't.

That night, my mom knocked on the door to my room. She spent a minute looking at all my trophies and posters up on the walls. Then she sat down at the edge of my bed, and told me how scared she was for me.

"Eddie, I don't care what that lawyer says. He could be wrong about everything. You could go to jail for a long time," Mom said, with her voice starting to crack. "You're still my baby, Eddie. I want you to have a good life. I don't want to see these things happen to you."

Dad came through the door as my mom started

bawling again. He got angry right away, and screamed at her for getting so upset. She tried to pull herself together, and started straightening up my room, and putting away my clothes. That's when she saw Marcus's jacket hanging on the doorknob to my closet.

She lost it.

"I don't want to see that jacket here again, Eddie. Get it out of this house, and give it back. I don't want to be responsible for having it here," she yelled through the tears, and ran out of my room.

My dad chased after her down the hallway, cursing at me for leaving the jacket out.

I took the jacket to school with me the next day. And I made sure that my mom didn't see me carrying it, either. I walked through the streets with it stuffed under my arm, and thought about all the good times me and Marcus had together. I wished that he was inside that jacket, walking next to me. I wished that I had never seen my grandpa's gun, and that we were a team again. But I squeezed that jacket inside my arm, and it was empty.

Most of the kids at school were just finding out that we had lost the game, and about the riot, too. They were coming up to me in shock, asking how we could lose. I told them that it was just a bad night for everybody, and that Aviation couldn't beat us again if we played them every day for a month straight. Then it hit me that Marcus would be sitting inside a prison cell before a month was up.

In homeroom, Ms. Randolph's voice came over the PA system, saying how proud she was of everyone who stayed cool at the game. She didn't say that there was a fight, or that the cops came. Instead, she just called it a "minor disturbance."

"I want to thank Coach Casey and the basketball team for reaching the playoffs again this year. They represented our school with dignity. I know that everyone is proud of them," Ms. Randolph said. "I also want to acknowledge the parents we honored at Senior Night. Without their support, our students would have to struggle much harder to achieve their goals. It's a pleasure to be part of giving something back to them in return."

I wanted to puke at all of that, because she didn't mean a word of it. She announced that I was the high-scorer for our team that night. And that I had played my last game for LIC and was going to St. John's next year. For the rest of the morning, kids talked to me like I did my part, and everyone else must have really screwed up for us to lose. I felt like a real heel nodding my head to that crap while I dragged Marcus's jacket around.

When I walked into English class, Marcus was up at Ms. Sussman's desk getting a load of work to do for after he was gone. I stood at his chair, waiting for him to come back. Everybody else was sitting down, copying the blackboard. I was standing out like a sore thumb. So I finally just hung the jacket over the back of his chair, and took my seat.

Marcus was halfway back to his chair when he saw the jacket. He stopped short, and looked like he was lost. For a second, Marcus turned his head towards me. Our eyes locked together. Then he turned away and fell right back into step. Marcus was already wearing a coat, and sat down with his back against the jacket.

After class, Marcus had his book bag in one hand and the jacket hanging loose in the other.

"How did they ever beat us?" he asked me.

"They didn't beat *us*," I told him. "They beat *me*. I was supposed to carry that game by myself. Instead, I got spanked."

Marcus asked me about Jefferson getting into it with Connelly. I didn't know a thing about it, and felt like I was at some other gym that night.

I tried to explain to Marcus about the jacket. But he

just waved me off. "Forget about it," Marcus said. "My mother's just on edge about everything right now."

I watched Marcus walk off to his next class. He carried the jacket out away from his body, like it wasn't a part of him anymore. I looked at him like he was already somebody different. Somebody I didn't have a handle on anymore. And I started to worry if *this* Marcus would ever give me up to the cops and say I was there.

Later on, I turned a corner and walked right into my mom and Ms. Randolph. They both saw me at the same time and stopped talking. Mom put her arm around my shoulder and kissed me on the forehead. Then she turned me to face Ms. Randolph.

"My son is really something," my mom said.

Ms. Randolph smiled without showing her teeth.

"I'm sure we'll all be talking about him for a long time," she answered.

Mom pushed me down the hallway, and told me not to be late for class. I stayed on Ms. Randolph's eyes until they got small and sharp, and she turned them back to my mom.

After math, me and Marcus went up to the gym for the final team meeting. I could hear balls bouncing and kids laughing from outside the heavy wooden door. They were already playing three-on-three. Everybody was smiling and ranking on each other with every shot that went up. There were boxes of pizza and sodas on the table in front of Casey's office. Big Andre was eating two slices at once, one on top of the other. He saw me and Marcus together and said, "Marcus, my man!" The two of them slapped hands, and pulled each other into a hug. Marcus grabbed an old ball out of the rack and started shooting on a side court.

I wasn't in the mood to play. Instead, I picked up a can of soda, and sat on the floor, up against the wall. I could feel the vibrations from out on the court running up my spine. I popped open the can and took a swallow.

The custodian came into the gym with his helper walking behind him. They took the blanket off of Jason's broken case, and started chipping away at the glass that was left around the edges. Marcus dribbled the ball in one spot, watching them work. Then the custodian pulled the white paper off a brand-new sheet of glass. The two of them lifted it up and fit it into the case. They rubbed out all the fingerprints on both sides, until it was clear and perfect. That's when Marcus went back to playing.

Casey stepped out of his office and blew his whistle. He walked over to the one section of the bleachers that was pulled out, and everybody followed. We all sat down. Then Casey climbed into the stands and sat right in the middle of us.

"For lots of reasons, this will be a season I'll never forget," Casey started out. "We learned what it was like to win together, and what it was like to lose. Nobody quit. Nobody went home. When it got tough, we walked out onto the court like a team. And when it was over, we walked off the court the same way. Even when they broke us apart, we stood up together and took what came. That's a team!"

Casey asked if anybody had something to add. That's when Marcus said what he knew about Jefferson. Kids hated Connelly's guts so much, they were just glad he was gone, even if Jefferson got caught up in it.

"Sometimes Peter's got to pay for Paul," Moses said.

"Then Peter must have been a black man," X said, looking right at me. "We always got to pay for somebody else."

Preston said that Peter and Paul were white, like everybody else in the Bible.

"Jesus was black!" X shot back at him. "He had woolly hair. Do you know a white man with woolly hair?"

"There's even a picture of black Jesus," said Andre. "My grandmother has one hanging in her house."

Casey just listened until all the talk died down. Then he said the gym would be open for another hour, and to take the food home that we didn't finish. On the way back to his office, Casey turned around and said, "Remember, seniors, I need your uniforms."

That really hurt. I thought if we had won the city championship, the school might let us keep our uniforms. I thought they might even retire my number. But now, some other kid would probably be wearing my uniform next year.

Marcus went over to his book bag and pulled out both of his jerseys. They were clean and folded, with the home whites on top of the road maroons. Then Marcus disappeared into Casey's office. He came back out a minute later without the uniforms. It was that easy for him. Marcus didn't play ball for LIC anymore. And Marcus wasn't the "Black" in Black and White anymore, either.

The jersey that I wore on Friday night was at home in a pile of dirty laundry. My road uniform was hanging in my closet. I just didn't want Casey to have to ask me for them.

Moses turned the radio up, and kids were playing games at almost every basket. I couldn't find a place to get comfortable. I didn't want to sit around and watch everybody else having a party. So I headed for the door.

The next night, my dad and I had to go down to Mr. Golub's office and make the last payment. Golub didn't get another dime after that, unless the case went to trial. Dad wanted me to be there to see him write out the check.

"Take a good look at what I'm spending my over-time money on," he told me. "This is the vacation we're not going to take this year."

Golub said the case against me was still weak. That after a while, the state might even drop the charges completely. It was a waiting game to see if I was going to crack, staring at all that time. The cops weren't going to quit, either. They had nothing to lose. They got to go home every night, no matter what. All they could do was get lucky and come up with somebody who said it was absolutely me.

Golub put a rubber band around my folder, and filed it away in alphabetical order. He said there was nothing left for him to do, except pick a jury if it came down to that. But that wouldn't be for another few months.

"We wouldn't want anyone who's ever been robbed

for one. We wouldn't even want people who've had trouble with high school kids in their neighborhood," Golub said. "And of course, we'd want more whites on the jury than blacks."

Dad said he was going to tell my mom that there wasn't any real evidence against me. And that the state would drop the charges by the summer for sure. Now I couldn't even tell her how worried I was. I had to pretend that everything was all right. I was as scared as I'd ever been in my whole life. And I couldn't tell my dad because he would have said that I deserved it.

My mom was always in my corner. I knew that she would stick up for me to the very end, even if a judge ever found me guilty. But I wondered if on the inside, she thought that I really did it, especially since Marcus had pled guilty.

I'd close the bathroom door behind me, and think how the prison cells on TV weren't any bigger than that. I even started leaving the door open a crack when I was in there, just to have a way out.

With basketball over, Rebecca wanted to start meeting up after school. I wasn't in the mood to scout any new talent. Besides, she had stuck with me through everything so far. And the more I thought about it, the more I knew I wouldn't want to see her with some other guy.

We were walking along the river on Shore Boulevard. All I could think about was the spot under the Hell Gate Bridge where I dumped Grandpa's gun. My heart was pounding and my palms started sweating the closer we got to it. I was holding Rebecca's hand when we reached the bridge. Maybe she could feel all of that inside of me. I stopped to look out at the water and thought I could see the exact spot where the gun hit. That's when Rebecca kissed me. She put her tongue all the way into my mouth, and curled it around my bottom lip on the way back out. A fire shot through me. But I wasn't sure what caused it. My eyes were shut tight and I reached both arms out around her. I held on until long after she was finished.

We crossed the street and started back through the park. When we got to the running track, I saw Marcus and Rose sitting together on a bench from behind. They were as close as you could get without being in each other's lap. They were talking, and Rose was squeezing Marcus's hand between hers. I swung Rebecca off to the side and changed direction in a hurry. No one but me saw anything.

I tried to push the picture of them out of my mind but couldn't. But by the time I got home, I could see them together. And it didn't bother me as much as I thought it would.

That night, Rose's cheeks were redder than I'd ever seen them. She did her homework in the living room, without saying a word to anyone. Later, she took Gotti out for a long walk.

My mom brought a basket of clean laundry up from the basement. She left it on the steps for me to carry upstairs the rest of the way. I bent over to pick it up, and my white home uniform was sitting on top. The 11 was staring me right in the face.

 BLACK

There were less than two weeks before I had to report to the DA's office. Everything that was finally happening between Rose and me was going to get cut off cold. I didn't know how that would change things. When you keep a cover on your feelings for so long and they finally break free, it's hard to put them on hold again. Rose said that it was just time, like all the time we knew each other growing up. But I couldn't imagine not feeling her heartbeat now, and how warm she was in my arms.

I wanted to tell Eddie about Rose and me. I knew that when everything settled down, it would be a bump he'd get over. But that good one-on-one feeling we always had was gone. For now, I didn't want to put one more mountain between us.

Rose didn't tell her parents. Her father would have put her under lock and key. Her mother was already walking a tightrope over Eddie. Something like this would have sent her falling for sure. I was

worried that when they did find out, I would be sitting in a prison cell upstate. Then they would be knocking me down all the time to Rose, and I wouldn't be there to prove I was somebody different.

I couldn't hold it against them. When they let me into their house, they weren't thinking I was going to pull a stickup with their son and fall for their daughter. Up until last month, the Russos were probably patting themselves on the back for showing a black kid without a father how a family was supposed to be. But my mother was standing up taller now than they ever did, even if you stood them up one on top of the other.

My mother had it figured out about Rose and me from the beginning. I was glad, because I didn't want to hide anything from her ever again. She didn't connect Rose to her parents or Eddie. My mother didn't even care that Rose was white. But she told me that people were going to keep hammering us for crossing that line. She said that's when we'd find out how thick our skins really are.

I couldn't hang out with Rose around school because of her mother. So we'd walk up and down Steinway Street, and stay in the library on Broadway. When the weather was nice, we'd go down to Astoria Park and sit on the benches. Rose would take a second look at every white sanitation truck that rolled past. She was worried that her father's buddies would spot us and tell him that a black kid had his arm around her. I just played it off because I knew that she was under a lot of pressure.

In math class, Eddie turned around to see me marking off a calendar. I had a circle around my days left at home, and a big X from corner to corner on the ones after that. He was looking right at it. It didn't make any sense for me to pretend it was something else.

"I got to figure out how to make the best of these days," I told him.

Eddie shook his head and said, "School's the last place I'd be. I'd—"

He pulled up short on his words.

"I don't really know what I'd do," he finished, almost one word at a time. "Only you know how it feels."

I spent as much time as I could with my mother and Sabrina. I helped Sabrina with her math home-work, and started doing more chores around the house. I made sure I was home for dinner every night. It was always important to my mother we ate as a family. Now I felt the same way.

"We'll always be a family. Time apart isn't going

to change that," my mother told us at the table. "We're going to take from this world everything that makes the spirit grow stronger. And that spirit will keep us from getting torn apart."

The things that were most important to me had changed. It used to be playing ball, and Eddie and me being big shots. Now it was my family. Soon there was going to be a wall between everyone I cared about and me. But that wasn't going to stop me from keeping focused on them.

I already missed seeing Casey every day. For the last fifteen years, Casey had coached eleven kids on the basketball team and forty kids on the football team. But I knew I wasn't just another player to him. When I handed in my uniform he told me he was still in my corner, no matter what. And that when I got out of jail, and college coaches called him about me, he would tell them that I was learning from my mistakes. He said I would be a leader on any team, and an example of how somebody could put their life back together.

I knew I'd always be tied to Casey through Jason. I'd never forget that Jason and me came from the same place, and wanted to do the same things. Jason lost his life, and I almost took someone's. Casey looked after the both of us as much as any coach could. Only I was still around to appreciate it.

I thought about Jefferson every day since he was transferred. I asked one of the officers at school if I could call him at his new post. But the officer said that Jefferson couldn't have any contact with students during the investigation. Things like that moved slow and would probably take another couple of weeks. So I asked the officer to tell Jefferson I'd see him again one day. And if Connelly ever came back, to tell him I said to go to hell.

I stressed, thinking my father would call on my birthday. Only I wouldn't be there to hear his voice. I didn't know what would be worse—my father finding out I was in jail that way, or him not calling for another two years and finding out from me after I got home.

I didn't ask for any money since I got out of Rikers. But for my last weekend home, my mother gave me twenty dollars and told me to spend it any way I wanted. It was impossible for Rose to get out at night. So I dumped any thought of playing ball at the Circle and took Rose to the Saturday matinee at Kaufman Studios. It was the first time we'd ever been to the movies alone. No Eddie. No cousins. It was just the two of us.

We walked all the way up to the theater and past

the parking lot where Sidney Parker got shot. I didn't want to cross the street to the exact spot. But I showed Rose where it happened. She wanted to get a clear picture of it. It wasn't something that I had to close my eyes to anymore. I could face what I did, and move on.

Rose picked out a love story, without any guns or violence. The theater was almost empty. We sat halfway back from the screen in the middle of the row, and shared a soda. I had my arm around Rose from the start. She leaned her head up against my neck, and stayed that way for nearly two hours. We watched all the way through the closing credits, until the lights got turned up.

On the way home, we stopped at the flower shop where Rose bought my mother's bouquet. I got her one red rose to remember the day.

"When you leave I'm going to press this inside a book," Rose said. "And I'm not going to open that page again until you get back."

That night, my mother went through the list of what she could mail to me upstate. She got a package together of things like toothpaste, socks, and underwear. Sabrina put her Walkman on the pile, and said she wanted me to have it. I never told her or my mother where it really came from. I held it tight in my hands and could almost hear that woman scream after we robbed her. I figured it belonged with me in jail. So I put it back on the pile and gave Sabrina a big hug.

The next morning my legs couldn't keep still. They were itching to play ball after missing out on Saturday morning. The Circle was always dead on Sunday. I shot the ball there by myself for twenty minutes. Then I jogged around to some of the other courts in the neighborhood, looking for a game.

The other yards were empty, too.

I headed back down 21st Street, ready to give up, when I heard a ball bouncing on the courts by the Department of Sanitation. I wasn't about to cross over until I saw for sure it was somebody worth playing.

Eddie had his back to me. He let a long jumper go from the corner. It went straight in, without even touching the rim.

I leaned up against a parked car, watching him. Eddie cut right and left with the ball. He hit shot after shot, wearing his maroon and powder blue Marauders. His stroke was as smooth as ever. But none of that mattered. I had his timing down from playing with him for so long. Maybe Eddie was carrying around too much inside him. He was a half step slower than usual. And it showed in every move he made.

I dribbled the basketball, crossing the street, and Eddie turned to see me coming. The D.S. was the first place we ever played together, and would probably be the last for a long time. I ducked through a hole in the fence. Eddie stood there with the ball glued to his hip.

"I was out looking for a game," I told him. "But I didn't think I'd find somebody this good."

"Yeah, I'm just good enough to get beat in the first round of the playoffs," Eddie came back with a straight face.

I tossed my ball off to the side, and put my hands out for Eddie to pass me the one he was holding. When he did, I pushed it right back at him and started playing defense. We weren't going hard in the beginning. And neither one of us said the score out loud after the first couple of baskets. So we didn't pay any more attention to it.

Eddie made an off-balance shot and threw me a smile. I got up tighter on him. And we both got more serious. I knew all of Eddie's moves and beat him to where he wanted to go on the court. When I was offense, I turned the corner on him every time. I pushed him to go faster and faster. But there was no way he could keep up, dragging everything around with him.

After ten minutes, Eddie needed a break. He was doubled-over, trying to catch his breath. I sat on the court with my palms flat against the ground behind me. Then Eddie followed. He took his hand off the ball and it rolled away. We were sitting face-to-face, with the sweat coming down the both of us. The rows of trucks parked outside the sanitation garage were quiet. There was hardly any noise from out in the street, either. And it felt like the only sound in the whole world was from our breathing.

There was nothing between us now, except for the line that separates black and white. Only I couldn't tell if it had been there from the beginning. Maybe it snaked its way through when we were too worried about saving our asses to see. I didn't know if it could ever get erased, or if we could find a way around it. I only knew that I wanted to try.